The Standing Ground

JAN FORTUNE-WOOD

Cinnamon Press
Independent Innovative International

Published by Cinnamon Press, Meirion House, Glan yr afon,
Tanygrisiau, Blaenau Ffestiniog, Gwynedd LL41 3SU
www.cinnamonpress.com
The right of Jan Fortune-Wood to be identified as author of
this work has been asserted by her in accordance with the
Copyright, Designs and Patent Act, 1988. © 2007 Jan
Fortune-Wood ISBN 978-1-905614-41-7
British Library Cataloguing in Publication Data. A CIP

Designed and typeset in Palatino by Cinnamon Press; Cover
design by Mike Fortune-Wood from original artwork:
'valley in the mist' by Tomo Jesenicnik, supplied by
dreamstime.com. Printed and bound in Great Britain by the MPG
Books Group, Bodmin and King's Lynn
The publisher acknowledges the financial support of the
Welsh Books Council.

Acknowledgements: Thanks to the Welsh Books Council for
their support and to everyone who read the manuscript and
offered criticism and encouragement. Thanks to the Arvon
Foundation for support and the space to write, to Jan Mark,
who sadly died in January 2006, and Celia Rees for their
invaluable criticism and suggestions, to Shanta Everington,
Stella Howden and Wendy Klein for their reading and
comments and to Geraint Lloyd Jones, my patient Welsh
teacher. Special thanks to Ann Drysdale for such meticulous
reading, and to my endlessly supportive family, Mike,
Rowan, Tamsyn, Cottia and Seth Fortune-Wood.

To all those young people who give hope for the future and especially for:

Rowan, Tamsyn, Cottia, Seth, Tanya, Jack, Louis, Kristoffer, Keziah, Bethia, Emily, Ayeisha and Finn

and to Ann for such generous attention to detial

The Standing Ground

1

In the shower Luke turned up the heat and closed his eyes, eager to wash away all thoughts of his awful day. Once dry he scrabbled on the floor for a t-shirt, flicking out the creases so that the smart fabric looked perfect. Drawers slid out from the wall as he pressed his palm to them. He grabbed fresh white boxers and jeans, pulled them on hastily and reached for the elecrostat brush; a couple of strokes and the memory style that had cost him a whole month's allowance sprang into shape, a halo of perfectly spiked black hair floating upwards from his flawless side parting. Idiot, he chided himself, much good did it do you.

Luke sank into a deep chair, closed his eyes and stepped through a virtual door, expecting to find himself in a familiar art site, but the site's background page had changed out of all recognition, replaced by what looked like an old-fashioned nature photograph. As Luke peered at the page a wall of mist reared up to engulf him, so that the stream and mountains suddenly disappeared from view. Luke had a moment of panic, but the mist cleared as quickly as it had come, spiralling above him and melting into a blanket of low, brooding cloud.

Through the clearing mist a girl of about his age stepped. Luke knew she must be the virtual guide to the site, but there was something strange about her that he couldn't immediately place. In fact the whole site looked odd, Luke thought. The girl's clothes weren't right for a start. She had on something bulky made out of a fabric Luke had never seen before, and her long red-gold hair was unkempt. It struck him as a bizarre way to construct a virtual guide. Who would want a virtual persona that looked like something from the Subs? She was pretty, though, Luke acknowledged, feeling another stab of regret about today's incident with Katie. Despite her odd clothes, Luke couldn't help thinking that there was something vaguely familiar about the girl.

'Cro-eh-so.' The guide said, or something like that.

'Sorry?' Luke's heart rate increased. Could he have stumbled into an illegal site from outside?

'Dim problem,' the girl returned. 'Sorry, I mean "no problem." I can speak in English. Welcome.'

The girl smiled at him, and Luke decided she was more than pretty. Get a grip, idiot, she's probably the virtual construct of some frumpy middle-aged woman from some backward country beyond E-Gov. She smiled again, waiting for a response no doubt. Luke tried to get his mind around the idea of a foreign site. She put her head to one side in a way that reminded him of Katie. He was sure he could feel the bruising on his ribs and legs more just thinking about Katie. He pushed the day's events out of his mind and smiled back at the girl.

'Interesting hair,' she said in English that had a lilt to it, some kind of accent. 'Is that how you really look or is it your virtual image?' she asked.

'The real me.' Luke grinned, regaining his composure.

'"Croeso" is Welsh for welcome. I'm bi-lingual. This is the real me too.'

'You mean you're not... sorry I thought you were... Welsh? But that... Isn't that a banned language?'

'Not where I live!' The girl laughed and flicked back a strand of hair.

Luke's mind crowded with a million questions, but he only said, 'Cool site.'

'I think so too.' Not one for false modesty then, Luke thought. 'It's taken me ages to superimpose it over some pseudy art site. I'm just squatting here,' the girl continued.

'Squatting?'

'That's right. I'm Alys by the way. Alys Eluned Selwyn, daughter of Geraint ap Tomas.' She laughed again.

'Right, pleased to meet you... er, Alys, I'm Luke. That's quite a name.' Luke felt his heart beating faster by the second. The girl had a way of holding eye contact that unnerved him. 'So you're saying this is an illegal site? How do you do that? Why is it illegal? What's it got that's so subversive?'

'Slow down, Luke. Any site I put up is illegal. I don't live under E-Gov. I live in The Standing Ground, Tir i Sefyll. Have you heard of it?'

'No.'

'Ha! Well, it's in Cymru, that's Wales to you. North Wales to be precise.'

'Why do you call it The Standing Ground?'

'Long story, Luke," she said. Alys lifted both hands as though she was about to conduct a symphony and Luke noticed a ring on her right hand, a knotted red-gold band set with a red stone. There was something familiar about the ring. Luke opened his mouth to ask her about it, but a sudden sensation of the ground shifting beneath his feet made him lose his train of thought. He was on a hill overlooking what must be a battle field. Wrecked bodies in mud-spattered mustard and red tunics were strewn across a plain. Luke was grateful that he wasn't close enough to see the details. 'Wales is somewhere that's been attacked and colonised for centuries, but there are always those who resist.'

The disorienting motion gripped Luke again and he found himself blinking into the murk of some kind of underground cavern. He shivered. Beneath his feet was the same black-grey rock that soared overhead; an immense cocoon of cold slate.

'When E-Gov came we vanished into the slate workings. There was an old saying. "Dal dy dir" It was revived as a kind of rallying call.'

Luke shot Alys a puzzled look. 'Literally "Maintain your land",' she explained, 'but more like "Stand your ground."'

'Ah, so The Standing Ground,' Luke said. 'So you don't live under E-Gov? Incredible! How come no-one knows about you? How do you live? Why don't they wipe you out? Do you learn history?'

'Slow down, Luke!' Alys laughed and flicked a strand of red-gold hair from her face. Luke decided instantly that Alys was not only vastly prettier than Katie, but perhaps the most beautiful girl he could imagine. Something in the pit of his stomach knotted and leapt.

'Sorry about all the questions,' he said, 'it's just... Crap!'

'I beg your pardon?'

'Sorry, I didn't mean you, Alys. My father's calling me for dinner. I must have been here longer than I realised.'

'Your father?' It was Alys's turn to look puzzled. 'I thought you lived in... those places with guardians instead of parents... what do you call them?'

'Pods. Yeah, we do. But we get to make visits to parents if we want to. I've got to go. Will you be here later?'

'The site'll be here as long as I can manage it, but that might not be for long. Depends how long it takes the owner to evict me. We have to keep moving our sites around anyway, to avoid being found by E-Gov, but even they can't be everywhere.'

'So why do you bother?'

'To let people know it can be different. We drip old knowledge into your world. Sometimes we manage enough maths and magic to sabotage minor E-Gov sites for as long as it takes them to put up defences. One day I'll crack their encryptions.'

The mist swirled around Luke again so that he felt dizzy. Strings of formulae formed in the mist. Through the haze he could hear Alys laughing and speaking words he couldn't understand, a musical torrent of hypnotic sounds. The mists cleared, and he was with Alys by a mountain stream, looking down on a tree-circled lake.

'I hope you'll come back, Luke. I'm not implanted like you, so I'm not always online, but you can wander though my pages. Visit King Arthur when you come back.'

'King who?'

'Come and find out when you've eaten.'

'Right, yeah, as soon as I can. Oh and … can I ask?' Luke began to frame a question about the knotted gold ring, but felt suddenly awkward and changed direction. 'Er… What's that top you're wearing?'

Alys laughed, 'It's a jumper, Luke. We don't have fabrics with memory or heat retaining properties.'

'What about antibiotic properties?'

'No, not that either and before you ask, no we don't smell. This is wool. We get it from sheep.'

'Amazing!' Luke felt like a wide-eyed five-year old, 'I mean it sounds really cool.'

Luke could hear Nazir calling more loudly from the kitchen. 'I've really got to go, but it's been great. I hope I'll see you again.'

Myrddin Emrys

Druids learn by heart and slowly, a lifetime of heart-learning. And above all we learn the strength of the human spirit. Tyrants come and go. They use the same weapons: fear, repression, lies, even death, but when we refuse to be afraid, when our souls are not destroyed, they wane. Druids are strong because we know that the human spirit is indomitable.

Where do I come from? From the mists of myth and history? From magic? From Carmarthen: the child without a father or the child whose father was called the Devil? From the wild woods, a prophet drunk on grief from all the violence I witnessed? I am all of this and none of it. Ambiguity has always been my fate.

I am not the king, but I am seer to kings: to Gwrtheyrn, also called Vortigern, the fool and the fox; Aurelius Ambrosius, who held back the darkness for a little while; Wthyr, his brother, whose lust was as violent as his sword, but who served his purpose; Artur, who like me, returns again and again, a light shining in the darkness.

They have all used my magic and now it will be used again and in new ways to let the tyrants know that our spirits cannot be quenched.

2

After dinner Nazir took Luke to his studio connected to the house by a long transparent walkway covering the whole stretch of garden. Tropical plants grew in there, and Luke never walked through without thinking of his mother.

'Her joyous garden,' Nazir remarked as he had a thousand times before.

Luke nodded. He remembered picking oranges with his mother to make juice on the mornings when he'd been allowed overnight stays from the pod.

Nazir stopped by the fountain. The screen at the fountain's centre was projecting what looked like a statue; the image of a woman seated in a coracle, a long sword balanced across her knees. It was modelled on his mother, Vivian. Luke dangled his fingers in the liquid; the water was real, and Luke kept his fingers in the cold stream until they began to burn with iciness.

'It never goes, Luke, the pain of it, but we're here to keep on living.'

Luke nodded and flicked the icy drops from his fingers. It was virtually unheard of for the babies of the elite to die at birth and even rarer for a mother of Vivian Raven's status to die in childbirth, but both had happened. Luke remembered picking oranges and figs with Vivian on the morning his mother had gone into labour with Inogen, the sister he had never known.

On every visit to Nazir's home, Luke looked out for signs of a woman's presence, but he had never noticed anything. If Nazir had girl-friends then at least he was discreet about it; no small items left in his house, no reports in the newspapers that were always bursting with celebrity gossip. Luke liked to think that if his mother had lived she would still be with Nazir. It wasn't something he would ever say out loud, of course. Life unions were not banned, but they were sufficiently frowned on to have withered to a minority occupation for eccentrics and suspects. This hankering for old fashioned families was just one more thing that made Luke strange; the kind of thing that would convince people like Tutor Simons that he should be medicated and re-formed.

The studio was a large Perspex and metal geo-dome at the end of the garden. 'So, let me show you what my glass tower is hiding today,' Nazir said, smiling.

The dome was taller than two storeys so that Nazir's towering art installations could be constructed and taken out by crane through the roof panels, all of which slid open and downwards. When the panels were set to clear the light flooded in, but they could be controlled so that some or all became opaque from the inside. From the outside all the panels were opaque so that the geo-dome looked like an edifice of black glass, important for keeping at bay the prying telephoto lenses of the art paparazzi.

'So here we have it,' Nazir announced with a mock flourish as he shepherded his son into the dome.

Luke gasped. The installation was the largest he had ever seen. 'It works like the fountains,' Nazir explained. 'Each tube is a plasma display panel, just like a computer screen. When it's turned on you won't see the screens, just the projections inside them, but this piece has a twist. One that I think you might appreciate, Luke.' Nazir put his palms together slowly, and then made a mock bow. 'Watch this.'

Luke moved closer. 'It's incredible.'

'Keep looking,' Nazir said quietly.

'Amazing! Who...?'

Nazir smiled and held up a hand like a magician at a children's party,'All in good time Luke.'

'Some of them look...' Luke searched for the words.

'As though they are not from our time?'

'Yeah! Can you do that, Dad? I mean this is going in a public space, in the middle of Victoria Square. Won't it cause trouble for you?'

'It's the fact that people won't know what they're looking at that makes it possible, Luke, ironic as that may seem. It's a kind of double bluff. Only the elite can access history so anyone who can recognise historical figures must already have access. Anyone who wonders what they are looking at won't find out simply by looking. Ergo no harm done as far as the authorities are concerned.'

'I'd give anything to have your kind of access to history,' Luke said.

'Ah well,' Nazir had a familiar smile that Luke recognised whenever his father was being deliberately

16

enigmatic, 'I'm afraid you wouldn't find access to a great deal of this even if you had the codes to the length and breadth of E-Gov.'

'So where…?'

Nazir tapped the side of his aristocratic nose and winked. Luke knew there was no use pursuing the subject. He suspected that Nazir must have access to foreign sites, but he couldn't imagine how Nazir managed to go outside E-Gov with the kind of surveillance that they mustered. His father might_be a celebrity, even one who travelled to other countries to have his work paraded as the pinnacle of E-Gov art, but surely they never let him too far out of their sight and hearing.

'But won't it make people ask questions they shouldn't be asking? They're not going to take kindly to that, Dad.'

'People already realise that they only have access to whatever their information quotients allow, Luke. They know it, but they live with it. I don't suppose most people will notice or care what they are seeing, but, in any case, I hardly think some petty Local E-Gov official can prove I intended to subvert the masses. I'm an artist. This is just what I do.' Nazir flexed his fingers and chuckled lightly.

'It's brilliant, Dad. That guy with the sword…'

'Ah, yes. That one's as much myth as history. King Arthur.'

'King Arthur? That's the second time I've heard that name today.' Luke bit his tongue too late. Nazir Malik might be the most subversive person Luke knew, but he was still trusted by E-Gov.

'How on earth did you come across King Arthur?' Nazir looked more concerned than angry, Luke thought. 'I don't imagine he's someone our friend Tutor Simons told you about?'

'There's nothing to tell really. I went to this art site after I had a shower and the er … guide mentioned that name, that's all.'

'An art site?' Nazir looked unconvinced, but there was an amused turn to his mouth.

'Well, I thought it was an art site. That's what's usually at that location.'

'You stumbled on an illegal site?'

'I think so. I didn't know they existed. Not like that, anyway. Me and Kyle have found the odd retro site with old films or music, but this was really different.'

'Oh yes, Luke, they certainly exist, and I think we're going to be seeing more of them. And this er... guide?' Nazir was smiling broadly now.

'She said she was real.'

'And did she say where she was from?'

Luke felt a sudden chill. Would his father collect information to hunt down people like Alys? There was more than one way to play at double bluffing. Surely not, he told himself. Luke could feel Nazir watching him.

'I'm not going to betray you, Luke, if that's what you think,' Nazir said softly.

Luke bit his lip. After the day he'd had at school he needed Nazir as an ally. His father's influence might be all that stood between him and a recommendation for assessment and behaviour modification. He had to be able to trust Nazir, but even so he answered evasively, 'She wasn't very precise about where she was from and a lot of it didn't make much sense.'

'Well, there are various possibilities. Some of the Trekkers are pretty computer savvy now, though many of them remain dogged technophobes. And there are a few people in the Subs who are getting pretty clever at hacking and dodging, despite the constant threat of Regulator Raids. Or of course, she might just be from The Standing Ground.'

'You know about The Standing Ground?' Luke blurted.

'As do you, Luke,' Nazir noted with a wry smile, 'And I hope you also know how dangerous it is to know.'

'Yes.' Luke felt stupid, but told himself Nazir had to be on his side.

'In particular don't say anything to Kyle. He doesn't have your level of protection, Luke.'

'I know,' Luke nodded gravely. It was a pity, he'd enjoy boasting to his friends about the cool girl he'd met online, but his father was right.

'So what did your Welsh girl tell you about King Arthur?'

'Nothing. You called me down for dinner.'

'Ha! So that's what took you so long. Come on. Let's get a drink and you can tell me all about the mists of Cymru and the other thing that is on your mind, too.'

'What? How do you know? Did you get a mind-call from school or from Claudia?'

Nazir shook his head and steered Luke towards the house. In the garden the projection on the fountain had shifted to a new image. Luke froze.

'You look as though you've seen a ghost, Luke,' Nazir said quietly over his shoulder.

Luke shook his head. The girl in the fountain was dressed in sweeping red and gold robes, not a bulky sweater, and she held a small bowl from which light seemed to spill, but it was obvious now why Alys had seemed so familiar to him, right down to the knotted gold band on the middle finger of her right hand. Luke took a deep breath and shook his head, 'I'm fine,' he said uncertainly.

In Nazir's sumptuous living room, Luke stood in front of the long wall that was taken up with a seamless screen. The picture, he realised, was of the same mountainside that he'd seen on Alys's home page.

'That picture,' Luke began, sitting opposite the wall, 'It looks just like The Standing Ground.'

Nazir put his palms together, raised his finger tips to his lips briefly and flexed his hands. It was a gesture that usually came before Nazir deflected some question he had no intention of answering. 'Quite a coincidence,' Nazir said. 'So tell me about your day.'

Luke would have to try to draw Nazir out another time. He began to tell his father about asking Katie Lomax if he could take her to Kyle's party. He galloped through the events quickly, not wanting to dwell on any of it.

'So after this boy, Bradley, told you that Katie does not go out with "Darky Messers" you swung a punch?'

Luke nodded.

'And naturally it was our friend Tutor Simons that broke it up and then initiated a flag of concern.'

Luke nodded again.

'Hmm. Well, don't worry too much. I'll have a word with your Connexions counsellor. I'm sure we can sort it out amicably.'

Luned

I am the one sprang from ancient myth. I am who I seem to be and I am not who I seem to be. I am Luned, mistress of the moon, who serves the lady of the lake. I am Creirwy, daughter of Ceridwen of the White Song, goddess of poetry who dwells under Lake Bala. I am the shape shifter who can guide the lost through the otherworld, Annwn, and the priestess who carries the vessel to bring healing and light.

3

Alys Selwyn woke, as usual, at 7 a.m. She stretched under her duvet aware of how cold the room was beyond her bed. She could taste the snow in the air, a thin, metallic bite. She turned over and remembered the boy she had met online yesterday. No doubt Luke slept under a thin cover that regulated its own temperature like the one Emrys had acquired on one of his many forays into E-Gov. Alys tried to imagine what Luke's podroom might look like, as pristine as some virtual environment on the web, no doubt. Poor Luke! All that luxury and he didn't even know who King Arthur was.

'History is always the first casualty of a government that wants absolute control.' Tomas Selwyn liked to remind his family. 'If people don't know where they come from they're less likely to object to where they're being taken'

The thought of her grandfather roused Alys to move. No doubt he would already be out in the poly-tunnel busy with his latest seedlings. Alys gingerly edged out of bed. At least the floorboards weren't as cold as the slate floor in the kitchen. She wondered what the floor was like in Luke's house. No, not a house, she corrected herself. Alys shivered. She pulled on thick woollen socks, grabbed a thick woven dressing gown from the foot of the bed and made for the bathroom, flicking a switch on the small electric wall heater as she left her room. By the time she'd showered at least her bedroom would be warm enough to get dressed in.

'Morning, cariad.' Alys's mother Gwen was a thin, busy woman with the same red-gold hair as Alys, though Gwen's hair was beginning to turn a yellow-grey at her temples.

'Morning, Mam. Is Dad out already?' Alys dipped into a bowl of oranges.

'Yes. He's gone to help Tomas, then he's going across to Môn for the meeting.' Gwen paused and let out a long breath, 'Owain's going with him.' Gwen sawed at thick slices of bread as she spoke, and turned to arrange slices of bacon on the stove griddle. 'Do you want an egg with this, Alys? You need a good breakfast, mind, if you're going outside.'

'Thanks, Mam, I thought I might go and help Taid.' Alys smiled at her Mother, 'You know I could get breakfast for myself, Mam.' Alys closed her eyes to take in the smells of the morning kitchen, the comforting salt-fat tang of the bacon, the smoky whiff of the coal stove by the old blue sofa.

'No harm in cooking breakfast, now,' Gwen smiled back, but she looked anxious, Alys thought. 'I'll be out at lunch time. I've got a call to make down beyond Talsarnau,' Gwen went on.

'Nothing bad?'

'Doesn't sound good, I'm afraid. Young boy.'

Alys nodded. In E-Gov no doubt her mother would have access to all the latest drugs and equipment. Gwen watched her daughter, handed her a plate of toast, bacon and egg and said, as if reading Alys's mind, 'It's a high cost to pay, Alys. We all want the best medical attention, but it's not worth our freedom, cariad.'

'I know, Mam. I hope you can help the little boy, though.' Alys carried her plate over to the table, a thick pine slab that had been in the kitchen since Tomas was a boy. Its surface was pale with scrubbing, hardened from the vinegar rubs used to clean it down daily. 'I want to put a new page up on my site today and see if I've still got my location, though I doubt I will have. I met a boy there last night.'

'Well, that's interesting. Did he bolt?' Gwen sat opposite Alys hugging a mug of precious coffee.

'No, he didn't. He seemed fascinated, actually. I couldn't keep up with his questions. He even asked me what my jumper was made of,' Alys said, laughing.

'Ha! You should tell that to Emrys Hughes! Tell him next time he makes a skirmish into E-Gov he can take some Welsh wool sweaters with him. Maybe we could start a subversive demand in old world craft items. It might make a tidy sum, at that!' Gwen took a long drink of coffee. 'Though I don't suppose jumpers would make as much as the underground software programmes Emrys sells to keep the ships coming with goodies like this coffee.'

'No, not that much,' Alys agreed, 'But you could be right, you know, Mam. People always want what they haven't got, especially something that's different. It might not bring the government down, but it could be another way of showing people that we're here.'

'Perhaps, cariad, though I suspect Emrys'll be more interested in this boy you met. How's the code breaking going?'

'I think we're really close, Mam, but we're still missing something.'

Gwen stood up and laughed. 'Well there's an understatement, Alys Selwyn, girl. I think what you are missing is a whole new mathematical system that doesn't exist, if I understand Emrys right.'

'Doesn't exist yet, Mam,' Alys countered. 'The government used to use one-twenty-eight-bit encryption to protect their sites till someone invented a new theory of algorithms to break in. They always said it couldn't be done, but it was.'

'So all you and Emrys have to do is invent another new theory of algorithms to break two-fifty-six-bit encryption and you can bring the government down?'

Alys grinned and carried her plate over to the sink. 'One day, Mam.'

'Well, here's hoping it's today, cariad.' Gwen looked pensive, as though she was about to go on, but she only said, 'Well now, I'd better get going.'

Alys pulled on leather boots and a dark blue waterproof. She wrapped a thick red wool scarf around her hood for good measure. Outside the door of Tŷ

26

Meirion, rain lashed the granite stones of the house. Alys hunched down and ran towards the cluster of poly-tunnels that stood across the yard and down towards the river. As she reached the door of the first poly-tunnel, she noticed how engorged the river was; another hour and the flood plain opposite would swell from muddy grass to a spongy lake. Alys ducked inside the first tunnel, threw back her hood and gasped as the warm moist air filled her nostrils and lungs.

'Morning, Alys,' Tomas called from the far end of the tunnel. He was stooping over a tray of seedlings, his hands covered in soft black loam. His weathered face reminded Alys of one of Owain's bark sculptures, craggy, but with the warm colour of pliable leather.

'Morning, Taid. Mam's gone to make a house call down in Talsarnau. She said she won't be back for lunch.'

Tomas nodded and went on gently lifting seedlings from tiny pots into bigger ones. 'Come and fill these pots for me, girl.'

Alys wandered down the tunnel and began packing Tomas' prepared soil into pots for the seedlings. 'Owain's going to Môn with Dad then?'

Tomas paused from his work and nodded, 'Yes Alys, it looks like we've got another politician in the family.'

Alys stood up and looked at her Grandfather. He looked older in the last few months, she thought. 'Isn't that what you want, Taid, for things to be the way they were when your dad was a child?'

'You can never go backwards, cariad. Whatever comes of all this it won't ever be like it was. It'll be its own new world. I want freedom, Alys, but how to get it, ah, now there's a question.'

'We have freedom here, Taid,' Alys said quietly, hoping her Grandfather would go on.

'We do indeed, but it's fragile. It'd be nice to wake up not worrying whether today is the day that E-Gov decides we can't be tolerated any longer, wouldn't it now?'

'Yes. But wouldn't it be even better to wake up thinking today is the day we bring E-Gov to a grinding halt?'

Tomas smiled, 'It's a thorny question, Alys. Your dad and his friends want us to be recognised as an independent country so we'll have security. They'll be putting the finishing touches to the European submission today. Then it's in the lap of the gods or at least on the tongue of Dewi Jenkins when he presents our case in Brussels. Then there's the likes of you and Emrys working away on the runes to tumble the whole thing to the ground.'

Alys laughed. 'Not runes, Taid, it's maths.'

Taid winked. 'If you say so, girl. Anyway, I imagine there'll be quite an argument between Emrys and your dad at that meeting.' He paused to pat a seedling down into its new pot, 'I suppose you haven't actually cracked the code yet then, you and Emrys?'

'Not yet, Taid, but we will.'

Tomas nodded, 'Aye, that'll be a tidy day. But you be careful. You tell Emrys Hughes to take good care with my granddaughter.'

'I will Taid.' Alys looked her Grandfather in the eye, 'So who's right, Taid? Dad or Emrys?'

'Ha! That's the question, Alys, but who am I to say?'

'Will it work? Dewi's submission to Europe?'

'It never has before, but your dad thinks we have to keep trying. Of course, in my dad's day the whole of Wales was one. We had a bigger population than Latvia then, but we lost a lot of people when E-Gov came.'

Alys could imagine how her dad would speak passionately at the meeting, arguing against Emrys, who would always be the outsider in many people's minds, despite having lived in Rhyd since he was a baby. Geraint's dark eyes took on an intense quality when he talked about politics, a look that Alys and Owain used to jokingly call his 'patriotic glaze.' These days Owain didn't joke about such things, Alys thought. Owain had the same look in his eyes.

Myrddin Emrys

The runes change, but not the quest. Once it was ogham marked on bark skins. Now it is mathematical symbols, software and art. The tools change, but the search is always for freedom.

What can I tell these good men who are in the grip of fear; these kind zealots who want to put up borders to protect their own? I will spin them a tale of resistance and courage and they will hear what they can.

And then we will go on doing what we always do, my apprentice and me; casting the runes, solving the maths, holding the light. In the old stories my apprentice learns until she outstrips me and that is as it should be. In one life she was Nimue, the lady of the lake, who some called Vivian. In that life she left me a prisoner in the glass tower. In another life she was Gwenddydd, my sister, who took on the burden of prophecy when I couldn't bear it any longer. And in another life she was Eluned, who could blend with the forest and find her way in the Otherworld of Annwn. Now she is Eluned again and her power is growing by the day.

4

Luke woke early, nightmare images of Bradley Hunter and Tutor Simons competing with a weird dream of Alys. She was with Nazir, of all people. They were casting spells into a mist that swirled into shapes, foreign letters that Luke didn't recognise or symbols from maths and algebra. Alys looked like some beautiful sorceress from one of the forbidden fairy stories Nazir used to tell him as a small child.

He opened his eyes onto the bright, sanitised world of the pod. The thought of Simons and the second flag on his record made his gut congeal. He blotted Simons out of his mind and closed his eyes, eager to connect to Alys's illegal site again.

It was still there, but there was no sign of Alys. Luke tried to tell himself it didn't matter. It was the site he was interested in, not the girl. He stepped into her King Arthur page.

'Croeso. Welcome.' Alys's lyrical voice greeted him. 'This is the story of Artur, the King who sleeps under the hill, who will return in our hour of need.'

An image of a gnarled hillside furrowed with exposed roots from a ring of giant beech trees filled the web-page. One root began to uncurl, flicking like a lizard's tail. Luke watched, mesmerised, as another root flicked free, a smaller one shaped like a claw. Another followed until finally, a thick stump lifted itself and turned towards Luke. The hollow shadows and worn bark metamorphosed into the head of a huge lizard, the bark-like eyelids peeling back to reveal sunken pools, bile yellow bisected by slits of black iris.

'Here sleeps Artur, guarded by Y Ddraig Goch, the Red Dragon.' Alys's voice said.

When he was small, Nazir had told him about creatures like these that had lived on Earth eons before humans. Dinosaurs, he thought they were called, but hadn't Nazir told him that they were extinct long before there were humans? He wondered if perhaps some of the creatures had survived into the time of King Arthur. How long ago had Arthur lived? Fifty years ago and a million years ago were as opaque as each other to Luke.

Y Ddaig Goch continued to rise. What Luke had taken for leaf mould unfurled; a membrane stretched across roots that were not roots at all, but the tapering, visible bones that spread through the creature's wings. The dragon turned one yellow eye towards him, fixed him and opened its mouth to let out a spray of fire. Luke jumped back and then felt stupid, reminding himself that he was in a virtual environment, but nonetheless he was sure that he felt a real spot of stinging flesh on the back of his hand where he had raised it to ward off the heat.

Another voice took over; an old man, Luke guessed, but with the same rhythmical pulse to his accent.

'There are many stories of Artur, each more legend than history. But somewhere far back, in a time when magic was the science of the Earth and people kept one eye on the sky in case of dragons, there is truth, not all of it history, but truth all the same.'

Luke wondered how things could be true if they weren't facts. He felt dizzy from the press of questions and wished that Alys was online to explain. He had a sudden sensation of sideways movement and felt cold wind. The dragon had tossed him onto its back and was carrying him higher and higher above a mountain landscape in mist, the raw granite pushing up through ochre soil. The dragon circled down towards a long timber hut. Something dark was spattered across the door. Through the shadows, Luke could make out the mangled shape of a slumped body, a shock of coarse red hair resting in a sticky pool of something.

The scene melted, and Luke was again looking down on the ring of beech trees. At their centre stood a man, dark hair to his shoulders and sun-weathered skin. His eyes were blue, intense like the back-light of an opal.

Luke jumped as the dragon spoke. 'The people who walked in darkness have seen a great light. The light shone in the darkness and the darkness could not overcome it.'

The man, Luke knew he must be Artur, was not tall, but he had a square set body that looked like it could be more firmly planted than the trees if he chose. Luke noticed that his clothes were the same as those in his father's image of Artur in the light installation, thick-soled, laced sandals, a leather tunic, reinforced with metal discs, and worn over a dull clay-red fabric.

A moment later Artur stood in front of a taller man in a small white-washed room. 'Hengst did us a favour when he killed the red fox, Gwrtheyrn,' the tall man said, 'but now his kind threatens to over-run us.'

Artur nodded, 'We won't always be able to hold back the Saxons, Ambrosius, but we may buy ourselves more time.'

Luke leaned in close to listen, but the site changed again. He was back with the dragon, the rhythmical wing-beats lifting him over a battle-field, close enough to hear the din of metal on metal and metal on bone. The banshee howls of pain as flesh pitted itself against steel made Luke's mind reel. On the ground, the clay was glutinous with blood and there was a tang that Luke couldn't identify, like having rusted iron pushed into his mouth and nostrils, so that he could hardly breathe for it. He was horrified, but fascinated. He wondered how people who lived beyond the reach of E-Gov without even the most primitive mind-enhancement could be capable of designing sites with such powerful sensory-wrap. Alys didn't even have proper clothing, so how had she built this site?

The dragon spoke again. 'The years after Artur killed Hengst were good years, but the seeds of betrayal had been planted years before.'

Luke found himself watching a young woman grinding herbs in front of a round hut, its roof made of turf. She reminded Luke of Katie Lomax, the same pale oval face, the same straight brown hair, except that she was a little older and wore even stranger clothes than Alys. The hut stood alone, perched on a steep hill. Luke listened to her chanting unintelligible words and felt a sudden surge of panic. The young woman looked up and Luke was sure she could see him. He shivered.

Inside the hut acrid smoke curled from a fire towards a hole in the turf and a black pot hung in the way of the flames. The woman sprinkled in her herbs and stirred. 'You must be hungry after losing your way,' she said to someone without turning away from the pot. A man stepped out of the shadows and the woman stooped to fill Artur's bowl with hot stew.

'No!' Luke shouted as Artur lifted the first mouthful to his mouth. 'Idiot!' Luke said to himself, 'It's just a website!' But he couldn't shake the feeling that he had seen the beginning of something terrible.

It was dark now, a kind of darkness that Luke had never seen before, so thick he thought he might be able to reach out and touch it. Inside the shadowy hut, drugged and spell-bound, Artur climbed into bed with the woman. Luke looked away. He found himself shaking, not knowing why he felt so afraid for Artur. Then the scene melted into the another.

It was morning and Artur stood outside the hut with the woman.

Her voice was bitter and breathy. 'You should know, Artur, that my name is Margawse,' Luke saw Artur's face twist with shock and disgust. She went on with a quietness that made Luke shiver 'I have waited all my life to take vengeance on you; the son of the beast Wthyr, who had raped my mother Igraine. You were the baby who stole my mother's love from me, the bastard of the man who killed my father. I have waited and waited, brother.'

Luke watched Artur clutch his stomach and sink to his knees, retching into the coarse grass.

The scene changes were becoming disorienting, but Luke seemed to have no control over what the site would let him see and neither could he pull himself away. He was with another young woman. She was dark haired and might be beautiful if her face were not contorted from crying.

'I have to go, Gwenhwyfar,' Artur said quietly.

'Leave me then, leave me to mourn our baby alone!'

Artur sighed, but stayed where he was.

'I'll tell you this – I'm right about them. They stole my baby to save one of their own. They worked some changeling magic on her...' Her tears stifled the words.

'That's grief talking, Gwenhwyfar.' Artur knelt down as though talking to a child, but he didn't touch her, 'I have to go. We are hemmed in. There's too much coastline to defend against the Saxons while the Scots flood in from the west. I...'

'Go then!' Gwenhwyfar spat at him, 'but you won't convince me. Those people are not like us. They move without anyone seeing them. You know they do.'

'But the little dark people are our friends, Gwe...'

'They are not our friends. They fight with you while it serves their purpose.'

She turned away and began to rock, crying more loudly.

Luke opened his eyes and realised his face was tear-streaked. How could Alys do that? Not only could he smell the blood on the field, but he could feel Gwenhwyfar's pain, as though he had been swallowed by her awful desperation. No other website could do this. There had to be more to this than sensory-wrap, but what? Luke gulped back Gwenhwyfar's tears and tried to calm himself while the site propelled him into another scene.

Luke stood next to a body. He felt appalled, but enthralled too. There was something more ghastly and more transfixing about a single corpse then there had been about the distant, gory mess of the battle field. Death, like blood, had a smell, the foul odours of bodily fluids and a sweet hint of decay. Luke had never been sick in his life before, he was aghast as the thin thread of bile spilled from him. He bolted upright, breaking the web connection.

'Luke! Luke! You'd better get up, you lazy Messer, or you'll be late for...' Kyle froze where he stood in Luke's doorway. 'Shit, Luke, what's that? You're... What it is it? You look awful...'

Luke blinked and retched again. He looked up at Kyle as though he had never seen him before.

'I'll get Claudia.' Kyle flinched away. 'Shit, Luke, that really smells.'

'No, don't get Claudia. I'll be down in a minute.'

Luke waited until Kyle had gone, then changed his clothes and took a deep breath, psyching himself up to face the day. Outside his podroom the world suddenly seemed too bright and ordinary. He glanced down into the sitting room below the mezzanine. It was empty; everyone else was already at breakfast. Luke padded along the matt grey grating and down the stairs. In the dining room the noise of chatter and scraping of cutlery on bowls threatened to overwhelm him. He slipped into his usual chair next to Kyle at the same moment as Claudia came from the kitchen carrying a tray.

'Good morning Luke, glad you could join us for breakfast.' Claudia had a way of smiling so that one side of her mouth reached higher. She was wearing trousers that matched the grey of the doors throughout the pod and a dark blue top almost the colour of her eyes. Claudia was everyone's favourite of the four Guardians in Luke's pod, but she wouldn't tolerate the reputation of her exclusive pod being threatened. He wondered what she would say about the trouble he was in at school.

'Do you want me to come with you to see your Connexions counsellor after the weekend?' she mind-called to him and Luke flashed a smile, relieved that at least she was talking through their implant links.

He shook his head, 'No, thanks. Nazir said…' He trailed away, unsure about mentioning Nazir's involvement, but Claudia nodded.

'Good. Well get it sorted, Luke, okay?'

Nazir

It was Vivian who first believed in my art. I met her when I was trading in software programmes with her father Gerard Raven, the most famous artist in E-Gov and my mentor. He pretended not to notice the time that Vivian and I squirreled away for ourselves.

This house was Vivian's and I came and went as I liked. She never asked questions, but when she became pregnant I wanted to stay. E-Gov frowns on such partnerships, but I was in favour by then and I wanted my son to know his father.

The doctors boast that infant mortality rates are down to one in a million, but our baby was that one; perfect, but stillborn. We buried his ashes under a stone in Vivian's garden. It was another two years before Luke was born, ox-strong and full of light. I had three more years with Vivian before I lost my muse and our baby daughter, Inogen, another one in a million. They are all here in this last piece of art for E-Gov, commissioned for Winterval. Four portraits in light: Vivian, Aubrey, Luke and Inogen, scattered among the thousands of images that will make up the tower of glass.

5

After lunch Alys climbed the two flights of stairs to her room. She stood at the window watching Tomas make his way back through the rain to the poly-tunnels. The wind had got stronger during the morning, pushing at the strong double plastic walls of the tunnels. Beyond their long piece of land that ran beside the river, the tall pine trees surrounding the lake bent in the gale. The sky was ragged, torn strips of sodden paper in a hundred shades of grey. Alys wrapped her arms around herself and rubbed herself to ward off the cold. Soon it would be Winter Solstice, what Luke would call Winterval.

The thought of Luke sent Alys to her computer. She keyed in the address of the site she had squatted on yesterday afternoon, and her webpage appeared. She smiled broadly; the slick interactive art site hadn't managed to load itself back in place yet, but squatting under someone else's web address was always a short-term game. She wondered if she might bump into Luke again or whether he had read the King Arthur pages.

She spent a couple of hours writing a new history page, and then closed her web files. She would have to try to find another squat tomorrow. She had a couple of hours before Gwen arrived home and she wanted to go over her maths notes again before she saw Emrys in a couple of days' time. Emrys had been teaching her maths since she was seven, but no-one except Geraint imagined that Alys was the pupil anymore. Together Alys and Emrys would crack the two-fifty-six-bit encryption; she was sure of it. Alys thought about her father and Owain. They were probably embroiled deep in argument with Emrys right now, insisting that independence was the only way to go. The task of cracking the code seemed more urgent than ever. She wanted to get there first, to give people like Luke a chance.

Alys was still working when Gwen opened her bedroom door. 'Hello, cariad. Aren't you freezing in here?'

Alys looked up. Her mother looked tired, her eyes more pinched than they had been this morning.

'How's...?' Alys began, but Gwen shook her head wearily. 'I'm sorry, Mam. His poor parents, they must be devastated.'

Gwen sat down on Alys's bed and Alys snuggled in next to her. 'How old was he?' she asked quietly.

'Ten.' Gwen put an arm round Alys and pulled her in closer.

'Could you... I mean if you had the equipment they have in E-Gov... could you...?'

'I don't know, cariad. Perhaps. He'd certainly have had a better chance.'

Alys stood up, her face flushed, 'I'm going to crack that code, Mam.'

Gwen smiled wanly and motioned for Alys to sit down again. She wrapped both her arms round Alys and hugged tight. 'We live in interesting times, Alys, as Tomas will no doubt tell us again over dinner.' Gwen smiled and stood up, 'Your room is like a fridge, Alys Selwyn. I don't know how you can work in here. I know we have to be careful while we're waiting for the new generators, but you can put the heater on to take the chill off you know.' Gwen spoke briskly, forcing herself to be positive after losing the little boy, Alys thought.

'I know, Mam. I just get so engrossed.'

'Well, put some heat on later before you go to bed or we'll have to chip you out of an ice block in the morning. Come and help me do some supper, cariad. There's only us two and Tomas tonight so I thought we'd do something simple.'

'Okay, Mam, but tell me about Emrys first.'

Gwen smiled. 'You know the story better than me, Alys Selwyn.'

'I know, but I like to hear it.'

'His mother was from Carmarthen. Somehow she managed to over-ride the tag that E-Gov had implanted her with and made for The Standing Ground with her baby son, Emrys. She always refused to talk about Emrys's father, which probably only made the rumours flourish, especially given Emrys's colouring.'

'But there are other black and mixed race families.'

'A few, but always a minority and there was always something odd about Emrys. He was always clever, even when we were small children; clever and different.'

'But you were his best friend?'

'Yes and everyone whispered that we'd get married, but that was never on the cards. We were always more like brother and sister. We even shared a birthday and we always competed to outdo each other in every subject, though he always had the edge in maths.'

'And he went away before I was born?'

'Yes, just before Owain was born actually, 2057. Disappeared without trace. By then he was bringing in trade with his software, but he was a lonely person, always on the outside. He'd always made forays into E-Gov. Sometimes he was away for months, but after six months people began to worry. They might have found Emrys difficult, but The Standing Ground would grind to a halt without his trade. Emrys was gone more than five years, but the trade continued while he was gone and gradually people forgot to be anxious. Then one day in 2062 he was back, a little older and I think a little sadder, but he won't tell a soul where he was or what happened. Now he comes and goes, as you know, and no-one asks any questions.'

'He's always gone on Thursdays.'

Gwen laughed. 'Well, he never surfaces on Thursdays, that's for sure, though I doubt even Emrys could make weekly trips into E-Gov territory and back, not without a nifty bit of shape shifting or the magic that the superstitious like to credit him with. Now how about that supper before I turn into an ice block in here?'

Myrddin Emrys

Coming home is a strange thing when you have never felt you belonged, but it was good to see Gwen again and to meet her children. I thought it would be her son who would become my little apprentice, the child who was born in the same month as… but it does no good to dwell on such things. Owain was a craftsman from the start, skilled and laconic like his father and like Tomas, but it was Alys whose mind was even sharper than Gwen's and sharper than mine. The Druids always said it would take twenty years to train the next generation, but by the age of twelve Alys could cast equations as quick as me or summon up spells in binary that would make the greatest computer wizard pause in admiration.

I came home, but I continued to lead a double life. I needed to learn more about E-Gov, find their weaknesses. It has always been like this for me, shape shifting and dissembling for the sake of the quest. And now I think we are approaching the end, or at least a new beginning.

6

It was Saturday before Luke had another chance to re-visit Alys's site. Luke had thought of nothing but Alys and her website for two days now. It was two in the morning, but Kyle was buzzing with adrenaline from his sixteenth birthday party and wasn't going to take Luke's hints that he wanted to be alone.

'Your father really is cool,' Kyle enthused for the thousandth time.

'Yeah,' Luke agreed non-comittally.

'I can't believe he got Sabre to actually play live at my birthday. Awesome! And his art…'

Luke yawned heavily, but Kyle didn't seem to notice. 'The way he had the band music bouncing off the walls in 3D quavers and crotchets and stuff. Inspired,' Kyle went on.

'Yeah, it was great. I think I'm going to get some sleep now.'

'Okay. I'm just so wired. And those screens he set up – I thought those tubular ones were brilliant and the miniature version of that fountain installation he did for the school courtyard. What's it called?'

'The Floozy in the Jacuzzi,' Luke said reluctantly, 'that wasn't its real name though, just what the locals called her.'

'Yeah, excellent and…'

'I need to sleep, Kyle! Get lost.' Luke grinned, but hoped Kyle would go this time.

'No problem. Night then.'

Kyle left at last. Luke wondered if Alys would be online, but she was hardly likely to be on the net at two in the morning. He sifted rapidly through the memory store of his previous visit to the site and found the point he'd reached in the story, so that he could call up the exact point on the site. He held his breath for a split second, anxious that the site might have been evicted by now, but the voice of the dragon picked up from where Luke had left off.

Luke was in a long cruck-built wooden hall. At one end a group of men were arguing loudly.

'You have the royal blood, Artur,' a dark haired, dark eyed man was insisting.

Artur nodded, 'Yes, and you know where I got it too. My father Wthyr forced himself on Igraine.'

'No one cares about that. Blood is blood,' the other countered, 'and yours is the same blood that ran in Emperor Maximus' body. Ambrosius was your uncle, what more can anyone ask?'

Artur allowed himself a small laugh and clapped the other man on the back, 'A lot, Bedwyr, a lot. The bishops…'

'Pah! Who cares about bishops?' Bedwyr made a face like he had tasted bad meat and spat.

'Many people, my friend. I'm for the Old Faith, and the bishops know it. They've grown powerful, and they'll never cast their vote for me. They will support Cador of Dumnonia.'

Bedwyr spat again, and cries of protest shot up from some around the circle. 'I'll speak my mind,' Bedwyr persisted. 'He's no warrior and a worse leader.'

'But his son…' another person spoke up.

'Perhaps one day,' Bedwyr conceded. 'He's got royal blood and a bit more about him, but you can't expect men to risk everything to follow a boy.'

Others around the circle nodded and grunted assent.

The scene changed and Luke found himself wrapped in thick mist. He put out a hand to steady himself and heard the dragon.

'In this time of uncertainty, Artur fought a great battle at Badon Hill. His enemies united against him, Saxons and new waves of invaders. It was a bitter and bloody fight, but Artur's light shone that day.'

The mists cleared and Luke was on a hillside he had never seen before. The grass was greener and the earth under his feet softer. Looking down he could see white lines sweeping the hillside. A moment later he was on the dragon's back and from a height he could make out the white lines as the outline of a galloping horse cut into the grass. On the eye of the horse an older Artur was seated on a stone. A cloaked and hooded figure, who reminded Luke of someone, stepped forwards, with a crudely made crown of twigs and leaves. A deafening cheer went up as the robed man placed the crown on Artur's head.

'Hail Artur, Lord of Arfon, Emperor of all Briton!' The robed figure shouted over the cheers. Luke knew that voice, but he must be imagining it. How could Alys have copied Nazir's voice for this image on a website? There was no Alys to answer his questions, and already the site was changing to the next scene.

Luke stood at the door of a whitewashed room that Artur entered ahead of him. In front of him Gwenhwyfar, older, but still beautiful, stood as though paralysed. Medraut's arms were around her.

'Is this the moment that Margawse raised you for, Medraut?' Artur asked, his voice cracking.

'I only wanted to expose those who would betray you, Father,' Medraut protested, but the sneer in his voice when he called Artur 'Father' gave him away. He had the same eyes and same cruel smile as the young woman Luke had seen drug and trick Artur.

'So the company of the faithful dwindled,' the dragon said to Luke. 'Years passed, five or ten perhaps, and the invaders kept coming.'

Luke was in another room where Artur tossed on a narrow bed. His skin looked grey and sticky. Two men spoke in angry whispers.

'We could have pushed the witch's brat back into the sea if you hadn't broken the line, Medraut.'

'You are not my commander, Cei,' Medraut retorted. 'Cerdic is confined. Hengst's grandson won't be celebrating tonight. You should be satisfied with that.'

'It is not enough!' The older man, Cei, raised his voice and Artur moaned on the bed. 'Cerdic is not only heir to Hengst, but Rowena's son. His father was Gwrtheyrn the Fox, giving him a claim to be Lord of Powys. He's here to take Artur's place. He must be killed or pushed back. Nothing less should satisfy you.'

'Perhaps Cerdic is within his rights,' Medraut ventured. 'There are princes of Cymru whispering that my father has abandoned his own people in favour of a Roman title. They say he's forgotten he is Lord of Arfon since that meddling druid proclaimed him Emperor of all Briton. He saves the English while the harvests fail in Cymru and the Scots threaten Môn. I've heard there are Welsh princes on the brink of an alliance with Cerdic.'

'And what about you, Merdaut?'

Medraut did not answer. He turned and stalked from the room.

In the next moment Luke found himself in the middle of terrible fighting, the iron tang of blood clogging his nostrils, the sound of men screaming and bellowing over the noise and reverberation of clashing swords. He stood a hair's breadth from Artur, but had the strange sensation that he was seeing through Artur's eyes.

A broad sword swung an inch from his face and Luke gasped as Medraut raised the sword for another blow. Father and son locked together; every sword thrust set Luke's body on edge with the jarring vibrations so that he thought his limbs might shake loose. Luke began to tremble; noise, smell and fear sent tremors of confusion through him, but he could not look away or leave the site. Something stronger than curiosity held him there. One blow sent Artur reeling, and while Artur tried to recover his footing, Medraut thrust his sword deep into flesh. The sky roared with thunder. Rain began to whip the earth. The ground was soon a quagmire of blood and torn flesh. Medraut, too eager to enjoy his triumph, lost his footing in the slimy clay and threw back his head in an attempt to regain his balance. He died before he hit the ground; his throat slit.

At Artur's side Luke heaved and vomited, but still he could not leave the site. The mist wrapped him again, and he was grateful for its thickness.

'Those loyal to Artur fought long enough for reinforcements to reach them from Constantine of Dumnonia.' The dragon's voice continued, 'They won the day, but Artur was too badly wounded. He lived long enough to name Constantine his heir. When death came, Artur's sword would be thrown into the lake and Constantine would know that his time of kingship had arrived. Finally, Artur told Bedwyr that no one should know of his death while the fighting lasted and no one should know where his grave was. The secret of where he is buried died with Bedwyr, but in our time of greatest need Artur will return.'

Once more Luke stood on the hill above the ring of beech trees. There was a ditch to each side of the trees. To one side the slope of the ditch was covered in tangled roots, but the other side was a longer, grassy slope. Bedwyr finished compacting the earth so that it would not reveal the tunnel that led to Artur's resting place beneath the trees. When he had finished the red dragon flew down and wrapped itself beneath the trees, its wings became like leaf mould, its limbs and claws like roots.

Luned

At night I watch the moon growing from a slender sickle as though it is something that I am slowly drawing on a screen pixel by pixel. It will be full by the eve of the Solstice and this year my power will also be full.

Last night I dreamt about Luke and Emrys. They were together in a garden, a beautiful, warm place full of blossoms, despite the winter, protected by a towering glass dome. I saw Luke dip his hand into the cool water of a fountain. At the centre was a statue that shifted shape so that at first it was a woman in coracle, Nimue of the Lake, and then it was a girl. It was me, Luned.

7

On Monday morning, Luke stood outside Natalie Thorpe's office pacing and waiting.

'You may as well sit down.' A thin-faced secretary with black hair that was cut long on one side and short on the other pointed towards the large beige chair positioned outside Natalie's door. 'Ms. Thorpe will be with you as soon as possible.'

Luke grunted a reply and continued pacing.

'Is it part of your problem?' the black-haired secretary asked testily a few minutes later.

'What?' Luke turned to face her and noticed her eyes were vivid green and veined like leaves. Expensive lenses for a Connexions secretary, Luke thought.

The secretary spoke deliberately as though Luke might be a little slow, 'Do you pace because of whatever condition you are suffering from?'

'I don't have a condition!' Luke bit his tongue before he went further and wondered if Simons had paid the malevolent secretary to wind him up before his Connexions interview. 'Paranoid,' he said to himself almost inaudibly.

The secretary smirked. 'You don't have a condition, you just talk to yourself?'

Luke opened his mouth, but thought better of it. He had to be calm for this meeting. He forced himself to smile at the secretary who had him fixed with her sharp leaf-green eyes. 'I'll just sit here and wait thanks,' he said, sinking into the plush beige chair.

The secretary curled her lip disdainfully, but didn't retort.

Luke shut his eyes and concentrated on his breathing. An image of Alys sprang into his mind. He'd tried to find her site repeatedly over the weekend, but she'd obviously been moved out of the squat. It could be anywhere or nowhere now; no chance of finding her again, but still she kept coming back to mind. Alys. Luke sounded the name in his imagination. The soft sound of the name reminded him of the lilt in her voice and the strawberry-soft colour of her hair. Her natural colour, not some artifice, he thought, glancing at the black-haired secretary. He shut his eyes again.

'Luke.' Luke heard his name and came back to the room with a start. 'Are you all right, Luke?' Natalie Thorpe looked concerned.

'I… I'm fine, thanks. Sorry, I was miles away.'

'Hmm,' Natalie said knowingly. 'Well, if you'd like to come in.'

Natalie seated Luke in another plush beige chair inside her office and then took up her position beyond the large grey desk. She was one of those thirty-something women convinced that they are completely in touch with what it's like to be a teenager. Luke imagined her keeping up to date with all the latest fashions, music and lingo so that she could 'relate' to her clients. She was certainly no Tutor Simons, but

54

Luke reminded himself that she was still to be treated with caution. She might be young, tall and what passed for pretty with men her age, but she had the power to have Luke medicated or even confined to a behaviour modification programme.

'Well, Luke, let me just go over what I know.' Natalie touched a sense pad on her desk. It lit up into a desk screen and Natalie quickly ran through the menu to find Luke's file. 'Hmm. As far as I can see, you are from good parental stock and keep in touch with your father, Nazir Malik.' Natalie said Nazir's name like she was tasting cream and smiled, the colour in her cheeks rising slightly.

Ugh! She fancies my father, Luke thought with distaste. He remembered that Nazir had promised to make sure the interview with Natalie went well. Surely Nazir hadn't... Luke thrust the thought of his father with Natalie Thorpe aside and tried to concentrate.

'Hmm. Right. You are doing well academically, but there is some concern about your attitude to authority, particularly in certain classes. Do you think your father has an effect on your poor attitude to authority, Luke?'

Luke sat upright, 'What?'

'Does your father encourage you to ask questions, Luke? I understand that he's an artist and I'm sure he is allowed a certain latitude, but that doesn't extend to you. If we feel that his influence is negative, we will have to revoke your visiting privileges.'

'No. I mean... No, it's not my D... It's not my father.'

'You were about to say something else then, Luke.'

Luke swallowed hard. He'd never slipped up like that before; he had to stay calm. If he called Nazir 'Dad' in here, then he might never get to see him again. He shook his head and Natalie pursed her lips, but didn't press.

'Okay, well let's assume for the moment that it isn't Nazir Malik who is provoking these bouts of unhealthy questioning, Luke. In that case, something else must be causing your poor attitude. Can you shed any light on what that might be?'

Luke shook his head again. He felt cornered. Had Nazir not spoken to Natalie or had their conversation gone badly?

'You have no ideas?' Natalie persisted.

Luke shook his head again.

'Perhaps there is a genetic problem, Luke. Perhaps you have this tendency to question things and be unco-operative because you share your father's artistic genes and sense of superiority? I understand people with this artistic genetic make-up can be very stubborn, arrogant even.'

Natalie's face flushed and she paused as though to steady her voice. Crap! Luke thought, Natalie Thorpe had come on to Nazir. Perhaps she had even gone so far as to suggest that Nazir should sleep with her in return for her giving his son an easy time. Luke imagined Nazir turning her down in that charming, but definite way he had. His stomach churned and he hunched down in his chair wondering if he was a lost cause. Crap, Luke, pull yourself together. Hadn't

Natalie just called him stubborn? He wouldn't give in that easily. He sat up straight and grinned at Natalie.

'Well, I'd like to think I've got some of my father's talent and good looks, but the questions… I dunno,' Luke shrugged and flashed his best grin, 'to be honest, it's just a bit of fun with old Simons. It's not like I'm looking for answers or anything; I just like to wind him up. I know I shouldn't, but it's hard to resist.'

Natalie stared hard at him, but then relaxed and nodded, 'So you're saying it's just normal teenage wind-up. Nothing more?'

Luke grinned some more and nodded. 'By the way, that's a cool pendant. I love the way it changes colour. You must be into light-art.'

Natalie leant back in her chair and preened. 'Well, yes, actually. Thank you, Luke.'

'If you like, I bet I could get you tickets for the launch of my father's new installation, the Winterval piece. I think you'd like it.'

Natalie brightened further. 'Thank you, Luke. That's very kind of you.'

She leant back towards the screen, but went on in a milder tone. 'I'm afraid I need to ask you about this incident on Friday, Luke. It doesn't look too clever, that kind of behaviour.'

Luke waited for Natalie to go on. He needed to play this carefully, not jump in with both feet.

'Would you like to tell me what happened. Luke?'

Luke shrugged, and took a deep breath. 'I asked Katie Lomax to go to a party with me and she said she doesn't go out with Messers.'

'Hmm, so you hit Bradley Hunter. I think I'm going to need a bit more than that, Luke,' Natalie smiled encouragingly.

'Okay. Bradley said Katie doesn't go out with darky Messers. Then he called me "Coconut Face" and asked if my mother had been colour blind or was she just pervy.' Luke could still hear Bradley in his head. He shut his eyes for a moment and slowed down his breathing. 'I hit him before I'd really thought about it and then I tried to walk away, but they all dived on me.'

'And did you call Katie names when she turned you down, Luke?'

Luke squirmed in his seat. He wanted to shout at Natalie to mind her own business, but he kept his voice even, 'No.'

'I see. So the five people who say you shouted abusive names at Katie and called her a racist...' Natalie glanced at Luke's file on her desk screen, 'Well, I won't repeat what you allegedly said, Luke, but you're telling me that those five people are all lying?'

Luke nodded glumly.

'Well, Tutor Simons seems to believe them, Luke. Can you account for that?'

Luke shrugged again. This interview was taking another turn for the worse and Luke's brain was racing, at a loss how to turn it around this time.

Natalie flicked a hand over the desk-screen so that the page dimmed and closed. She leaned back in her chair and sucked in air, watching Luke closely. 'Let's just say I believe you, Luke. That still leaves us with a problem.'

Luke waited.

'The thing is, Luke, it doesn't explain why Tutor Simons and some of the other teachers are so ready to believe the worst of you. I know you told me that your questions in class are just a wind-up, but I'm paid to dig a bit deeper than that, Luke.'

Luke sighed heavily and fidgeted in the plush beige chair.

'So, what I'd like you to do is to complete one of my attitude tests and don't try to fake it, because it's far too complex for you to guess the so-called right answers consistently and I'll know if your answers don't match one another. Do you understand?'

Luke nodded.

'Good. I'll ask Jodie to show you to an interview room and explain what we need you to do. You'll log on to a webpage that you're directed to, and then our virtual version of Jodie will guide you through the questions.'

Luke cringed at the idea of being trapped with virtual Jodie for the next hour or more while she tried to confuse him into displaying all the wrong attitudes to gauge his Connectivity fitness levels.

'I'd like you to come back on Thursday morning, Luke, and we'll go over your results and decide how best to move forward.'

After the interview Luke wandered to the school café to find Kyle. He didn't want to eat lunch, but he didn't want Bradley and the Beauts thinking he was too churned up from the meeting with Natalie to show his face. Katie and her friend Tess were sitting at the table by the door to the café so that he had to walk past them as he entered. He put his head down and tried not to notice their sniggers or the whispers of 'Darky' and 'Coconut Face' as he edged past them. One thing was certain, he was over Katie Lomax. She didn't even seem pretty now that he'd met Alys. He gave himself a mental kick. You'd better get over Alys, as well, dumbo, it's not like you're ever going to see her again, or ever at all in real life.

Luke slumped into a chair next to Kyle.

'You all right?' Kyle asked.

Luke nodded, 'Have to take a test.'

'Shit!' Kyle sympathised, his mousy brown hair flopping unfashionably onto his face.

'Have to go back on Thursday,' Luke added.

'You getting lunch?' Kyle asked. He looked uneasy, as though he was under suspicion himself. Luke couldn't blame him. Kyle hardly needed to be seen hanging out with a Tagger, which was what Luke was in danger of becoming after Thursday.

'Not hungry,' was all Luke said.

Kyle leaned closer and lowered his voice, 'Do you think they'll…'

Luke shrugged.

'Shit!' Kyle said again. He leaned back in his chair as Bradley, Charles and Sam walked past their table.

They stopped as a group, and Luke wondered if Bradley was mind-calling marching orders to the other boys, which would be just his style. They turned and faced Luke with the same synchronised precision. Definitely having their strings pulled, Luke told himself, waiting for their sarcastic comments.

Bradley swung round to face Charles and Sam, 'You two smell anything?'

Bradley's groupies raised their noses on cue. Bradley sniffed more loudly, 'Can't quite place it,' he went on, admiring his own performance and beginning to draw glances from other tables. 'No… ah, yes… I've got it, of course, a kind of medicinal smell. The sort of smell Taggers give off.'

Luke hunched down in his seat resisting the urge to throw another punch at Bradley. He could see Kyle glancing at him anxiously. 'Let it go, Luke,' Kyle mind-called.

'Don't worry,' Luke called back, 'I won't give him the satisfaction.'

Kyle visibly relaxed.

'So which Tag is it that you're being treated for?' Bradley persisted. 'Let me guess… Questioning Authority Disorder maybe or perhaps it's Inappropriate Behaviour Syndrome. I hear the drugs for that are a real trip as long as you don't mind the drooling.'

Luke gritted his teeth and turned to Kyle, 'So, great party on Friday or what?'

Bradley sneered and turned away with Sam and Charles.

'Shit!' Kyle said for the third time when the Beaut boys were out of ear-shot. 'Nice going, Luke. Even I wanted to punch his lights out.'

Luke let out a long, slow breath, 'Thanks, let's just hope he's still wrong on Thursday, eh?'

Myrddin Emrys

Grief is a terrible curse. In that life I wandered for fifty years, blind with grief after the loss of my brothers. Now I wander between two lives, grieving for my mother in one life and for my lover and children in another. At the council on Môn I could see the grief on the faces of those arguing against me. They have all lost people to E-Gov and the grief shows.

Dewi Jenkins has gone to Brussels to plead their case. They do what they must and I will do what I must. I know the light will shine in the darkness again. I know he will return, and he will be guided by the one who can find the way through Annwn.

8

'Penny for your thoughts.'

Alys looked up and shook herself like a cat sluicing off Welsh rain. 'Sorry Emrys, I was miles away.' Alys sucked in her lower lip and stared at the board covered in formulae and notes propped in front of her.

'That's all right, Alys. My mind's beginning to do somersaults as well. We'd better call it a day. Sufficient unto the day are the evils thereof, as Tomas would say.'

'Do you think we'll crack it, Emrys?'

Emrys stood up and stretched. The fire in the wood-burning stove had gone out hours ago while they were poring over numbers and configurations. Outside, the wind was beginning to make a shrill noise like migrating insects. Emrys felt suddenly cold and tired. He looked at Alys for a moment. Her bottom lip was still sucked in, in that way she had when she was concentrating hard or puzzled by something. She'd been doing that since she was a precocious seven year old demanding that he teach her real maths. Emrys reminded himself that he'd achieved a great deal. It was the money he made selling programmes on the underground market that enabled the people of The Standing Ground to trade. Without it Gwen Selwyn wouldn't get the drugs she needed to treat her patients or the coffee she needed to keep her spirits up. So much achievement, but still…

'Do you Emrys, do you think we'll ever crack it?' Alys asked again, bringing Emrys back to the cold room and dark, wet day in December.

'We'll crack it, Alys, but that's not really what you're asking is it, girl?' He had long since learnt not to patronise Alys with half truths. 'What you want to know is will we crack it in time, eh?'

Alys nodded, pushing back a strand of red-gold hair.

'Honestly, Alys, I can't say. If Dewi Jenkins carries the day in Brussels then we don't have long, that's for certain, but who knows how things will go?'

'They've got more support in Brussels than they used to have, haven't they? Dad says that since our trade figures have gone up, more of the smaller European countries are willing to back us. Owain reckons several of the bigger countries will vote for our independence as well, to get back at E-Gov after they opted out of Treaty commitments in the last Convention.'

Emrys nodded and wandered over to the porcelain sink. He poured water into a stove top kettle blackened with use and took it to the wood-burner.

'Pass me that kindling, would you Alys.' Emrys busied himself with the fire for a few minutes then straightened again. 'I don't know, Alys. Dewi and your dad have more of a finger on the pulse when it comes to Brussels. Politics has never been my game, I'm afraid; not that kind anyway. All I know is if they succeed, and we become independent, then our little maths sessions would become E-war instead of subversion.'

Alys looked hard at Emrys and coloured. 'Emrys?'

'Go on.'

'You didn't vote for independence did you?'

Emrys began to laugh. 'Alys Selwyn!'

'I'm sorry. It's just, well…most of the reason we've got other countries to support independence is because of the trade figures and that's mostly down to you.'

Emrys laughed. 'Much as I'd like to take sole credit for all the wealth of The Standing Ground, I hardly work single handed, Alys.'

'But you…'

'Me? I'm brilliant, girl, bloody brilliant! But I didn't get into selling programmes round the world so that Y Tir could get more political leverage. I trade so that we have the things we need to live. We'd be a subsistence economy without the ships coming into Caergybi.'

'So you voted against?' Alys pressed, grinning.

'Yes, Alys Selwyn, I voted against, and I'm surprised your dad let you come here tonight after the set to we had at Môn. I'm going to have something to eat. You hungry?'

'Starving,' Alys confirmed. 'Can I cook?'

'If you like. I've got some of your dad's bacon in the fridge and Tomas' tomatoes.'

'Right.' Alys sauntered into the kitchen area of Emrys's long downstairs room and began pulling ingredients out of his fridge. 'Dad knows better than to try to stop me coming here,' she said, layering bacon onto a pan. 'He'd have Mam to answer to as well as me.'

Emrys smiled and nodded. The Selwyn women had always been a powerful breed, more powerful than Alys realised, Emrys thought. 'What about Tomas? Where's he stand in all this?'

'You know Taid; he's keeping his peace, not taking sides. He wants independence I think, or at least he wants security, but I don't think he likes the thought of giving up on the people outside the Ground. Taid likes to be on everybody's side.'

'Ha! Now there's an achievement. Still, I don't blame him not wanting to dive into the argument.'

Emrys watched Alys while they were eating. If she knew, then she showed no signs of it. He wondered. 'Tell me something, Alys, the new ideas we tried out today, tell me how you thought of them.'

Alys coloured and paused. 'I dreamed them.'

Emrys nodded.

'You dream answers too?' Alys asked eagerly.

'Sometimes, though it's more daydreams with me. I just had a hunch that you might.'

'Why?'

''Cos you're Gwen's daughter.'

'I dreamt about you the other night.'

'Did you now?'

'Yes,' Alys looked directly into Emrys eyes, the darkest eyes of anyone she knew, 'You were with that boy I told you about, Luke.'

Alys thought she noticed Emrys's pupils dilate before he smiled nonchalantly. 'Now there's a dream to conjure with. I'll make some tea before I drive you home, eh?'

Nazir

'Enchanting.' I hear it all the time from women like Natalie. They say it without a trace of irony. It's the least I can do, but I'm not sure whether this particular enchantment will be a strong enough spell to save him. This fight will be his.

And while he prepares for the great battle I will go on fine-tuning my enchantment: I have conjured so many images in light now. My family first, including my Indian father who died before I was born and who the children I grew up with liked to call a black devil. Then the rest: figures from history and from myth and from the mists where those two meet. They are all there, the great and the good, the archetypal and the forgotten. When I flick the switch the installation will shimmer with coloured bubbles that soften to transparent globes, each containing the image of someone who has lived or someone whose story was so towering that it was as though he lived. Each image will constantly change to another, shape-shifting through time and space.

9

Leaf-eyed Jodie looked as humourless as always when Luke arrived for his second interview with Natalie.

'You'll have to go away and come back in half an hour,' Jodie told him in her clipped officious voice. She leant over her desk as though she was busy studying something closely, but Luke could see that her desk screen wasn't activated. 'Are you still here?' she asked testily from behind her curtain of black hair.

'It's not really worth going to class for half an hour,' Luke reasoned, 'I could wait in the chair. I won't pace. I've got some websites I want to visit, so you won't even know I'm here.'

Jodie fixed him with her veined green eyes and spoke slowly. 'You can't wait here. Go away and come back in half an hour.'

Luke grinned and sauntered over to the chair outside Natalie's office door. Jodie stood up, as though startled. 'Leave!'

Luke almost jumped. She really didn't want him around then. He started to walk away, and then stopped. There were two voices inside Natalie's office, and he would swear one of them was... Nazir? Had Natalie told Jodie to make sure Luke went away so that he didn't see Nazir leaving her office? Luke grinned quickly at Jodie, 'No problem, I'm out of here.'

In Natalie's office half an hour later, Luke tried to look composed as Natalie activated his file. She pursed her lips and let out a long stream of air.

'Hmm. Well, Luke, I should tell you that there are some trends in your test that give me concerns. Frankly, I think you do have an over attachment to your father. I shouldn't have to tell you, Luke that E-Gov makes sure that society works in everyone's best interests and it's not in your best interests to be over familiar with a birth parent. You do understand that, don't you?'

Luke nodded.

'Hmm.' Natalie eyed Luke closely. 'I need to know you really understand what is in your best interests, Luke. Can you explain to me why E-Gov has pronounced that your individual will is so bad for you?'

Luke nodded, 'Of course. Individual Will leads to chaos.'

'Quite.' Natalie pursed her lips again, 'And the General Will?'

'Is what all right-thinking people really want. Deep down we all want what's in our best interests, but we only get that by abiding by the General Will, not by being seduced by our individual desires. E-Gov rationally discerns the General Will so it would be irrational and wrong thinking not to accept it,' Luke said with as much conviction as he could muster.

'Very good, Luke, but do you believe any of that?'

'Of course,' Luke swallowed hard.

'That's what I need to hear from you, Luke.' Natalie flashed a sudden smile and relaxed for a moment. She touched her screen and brought up a new page. 'I'll tell you what I'm going to do, Luke.'

Luke felt every muscle in his body tense; the world seemed to go completely quiet.

'I'm going to help you to make sure that you really believe it. I want to be convinced that your inappropriate questions are just high spirits and that you are not going to persist with them. I need to be sure that you accept the General Will as laid down by E-Gov and that you are not hankering after some never-never land where children live with birth parents, and people are exposed to all kinds of dangerous ideas that only do them harm. So, I've arranged for you to meet someone who used to ask the same sort of questions as you. His name's Billy, and now that he realises how wrong he was, he's been assigned to assist me with counselling cases like yours, Luke.'

Luke stifled the urge to object to being called a 'case' and let out a sigh of relief. At least this was a reprieve, he told himself.

'After you've had a chat with Billy, we'll meet up again and see if we can't put this whole incident behind us. Does that sound reasonable?'

Luke nodded again, 'Yes, I mean… thank you.'

Myrddin Emrys

People will not stir into protest and prophecy while they have their bread and circuses, but only when they are under threat; only when they begin to feel their losses.

It is time for my apprentice to come into her own. She is Luned and Creirwy and so much more. She does not know the extent of her own power yet, but she begins to dream. She begins to make real what she imagines. She conjures the Otherworld, Annwn, and she will guide the boy through it.

10

Alys woke early. The air in her room was cold, even colder than usual. She extended her tongue into the air and breathed in, a slight bitterness on the chill air. It must be snowing. She pulled the duvet around herself and shivered, steeled herself, then threw back the cover and stepped onto the polished floorboards. From her window she could see the first snowfall, a deep crust of iced sugar that turned the poly-tunnels into long igloos. The snow was still falling, a thick blur of white spirals buffeting their way to the frozen ground. It was just as well she had seen Emrys yesterday. There would be no journeys today.

In the kitchen Tomas knelt by the stove coaxing kindling to light.

'Quite a fall out there, Alys,' Tomas nodded towards the window, which faced the same direction as Alys's bedroom, towards the garden and stream. 'There's tea in the pot,' Tomas said, still concentrating on the fire, 'Need to keep warm today.'

Alys padded over to the table, her thick woollen socks making a soft sandpaper sound on the slate floor, 'Thanks, Taid. The snow does look deep. Beautiful, though. Shall I pour you some more tea?'

Tomas straightened and rubbed his back. 'That'll be lovely,' he said, nodding, 'That's one job done to start the day.' He was bulked out in fleece lined trousers and thick sweater, ready for a morning in the poly-tunnel, but Alys could see from his neck and wrists that he was thinner lately. Tomas took a long gulp of the hot tea and sat down next to Alys.

'You're up early, girl.'

'Hmm. I think it's this encryption, Taid. My brain won't let me rest.'

Tomas laughed lightly, 'You want to watch that, you know. Just like your Mam. Once she's got an idea there's no letting go with Gwen.'

Alys laughed in return. 'What, Mam's the stubborn one and Dad just gives in?'

'Ah well, I know he's been a bit like a dog with a bone with all this politics, but when it comes to it...' Tomas stopped for less than a moment, but Alys saw the slight wince.

'Are you all right, Taid? Shall I get Mam?'

'No cariad, Gwen'll be up and about the day soon enough. Don't you fret about me.'

Alys bit her lip and studied Tomas, but knew better than to press the matter. 'Mam won't be able to get far to see people today. I think she could do with the rest, though. Can I get you some breakfast, Taid?'

'Lovely. How about a bit of bacon, cariad?' Tomas leant his head on hands locked together beneath his chin, 'You're right about Gwen. She works too hard. Dedication, that's what the two of you have in common, good at the long haul the two of you are.'

Alys smiled and began arranging ingredients for breakfast. She breathed in the smells as she worked: the comforting fat from the bacon, the sharp citrus tang of oranges as she halved and squeezed them.

When breakfast was ready, Alys laid out plates and cutlery and two long glasses of orange juice. 'Tell me what it was like before E-Gov, Taid,' she said as she sat at the table opposite Tomas.

Tomas smiled and took a long drink of orange juice. He began sawing at thick slices of bread and bacon. 'The seeds were being sown when I was a baby, cariad, not that many people took much notice. There were a few voices raised in the wilderness, but most people thought they were cranks. People were too busy getting on with their lives to realise what was happening.' Tomas paused to take a mouthful of breakfast, 'Nice bit of bacon, now.'

'So they introduced all the changes without people protesting?'

'Well there was the odd protest, or so my dad told me. One group started a campaign to stop identity cards. Some people campaigned against a war the government had got embroiled in.'

Alys nodded, 'But children still lived with their parents, Taid?'

'They did, cariad. That was another right that disappeared by stealth. They started with all these campaigns about caring for children. All very emotional stuff, the sort of thing no-one wanted to argue with. Then they brought in this law that was apparently to protect children, and no right thinking person could disagree. A database of all the children. It

76

sounded good, too, except it meant any pervert who happened to be a children's worker could search for vulnerable children in their area, no problem. And it was nothing to do with protecting children really. They wanted to prove they could write the software to run the thing, that's all, so they could sell the computer programmes to the rest of Europe.'

'So what happened next?'

'Well, they were telling people that they were helping all these children, saving them from their parents. Bit by bit, parents lost confidence and the government dripped away at the message that the home wasn't really a safe place. They started opening schools longer and longer hours till in the end most parents were lucky if they spent twenty hours a week with their own children. By the time full E-Gov was running around 2020 the talk was all about how no right thinking person could imagine that the home was the best place for any child.'

Alys shivered, 'And history?'

'Some toe-rag in the government had the bright idea we should teach what he called "citizenship history". It wasn't a big step from that to banning history teaching altogether except for a few edited morsels that I believe E-Gov still peddles.'

'So what was different here, Taid?'

'Resistance, Alys girl, resistance. The Scots made a tidy move early on. They saw it coming and got their independence. We weren't as quick. We stood out against some of the policies, but there were splits in the Assembly and soon it was too late.'

Tomas moved the uneaten food around his plate and finished his orange juice. 'Think I'll put the kettle on and make some more tea to take over to the tunnel. Do you want anything else?'

'No thanks, Taid, I might make some chocolate in a bit. Aren't you going to eat the rest of your breakfast?'

Tomas eased himself into standing position and Alys bit her tongue as he winced again and put a hand quickly to his side.

'Oh, that's plenty for me, Alys.' Tomas said lightly, changing the subject, 'E-Gov tried to evacuate these villages up here in 2030, when your dad was just a toddler. Forced relocations. That's not that they called it, of course, but people went to ground in the slate mines or took to half-derelict villages tucked away in the hills. E-Gov didn't get very far with their relocation plans. Once they'd backed off, others joined us: people making a bid for freedom while they had the chance, before mass implants meant they could track everyone in England and South Wales.'

Tomas stopped talking and stared into the steam rising from the kettle so that Alys wasn't sure whether it was steam or a stray tear misting his brown eyes. 'We had some hard winters in those years, hiding away in the bowels of the Moelwyns. Lost some good people.'

'Like Nain?' Alys asked gently.

'Yes, cariad. Your dad was only three when his mam died. Useless waste of life and here I am still doddering on.'

Alys laughed softly, 'You're hardly doddering, Taid, and seventy-two's not such an old age these days.'

'Ha! I'm no spring chicken. Now, I'd best be off to the tunnel, cariad. You let Gwen know I've had breakfast.'

In her room, armed with a steaming mug of hot chocolate and a warm wool carthen thrown over her shoulders, Alys hunched over the key board and began to type new pages into her website.

'Shheesh! How do you work in this cold?' Owain's voice cut through the silence and Alys jumped at the sound.

Outside it was long since dark. She rubbed her arms, swathed in layers of clothing and grinned at her brother, 'Made of strong stuff, I am.'

'Mam says dinner's nearly ready.' Owain peered at Alys's computer screen and wrinkled his nose, 'That code cracking?'

'No, Emrys found this site in a government archive with only the old 128-bit encryption. It's from when Taid was a toddler. I can't understand why more people didn't resist.'

'Don't suppose they saw it coming.'

'Perhaps they didn't, but that's the problem with setting up new systems, Owain. You have to think about whether the people who come after you might abuse your system to control peoples' lives.'

'You should just come right out with it, Alys Selwyn, say what you mean.' Owain had his hands jammed into the pockets of his dark wool trousers, his feet planted apart. 'What if you and Emrys never break the code, Alys? Why should we give up the chance of freedom for our own people on the off-chance that you and Emrys Hughes might save the whole world one day?'

Alys squared up to Owain. She was shivering. She tried to steady herself so that Owain wouldn't notice the shake in her voice. 'I don't know if I hold with "our own people" Owain. What does it mean, anyway? That we only care about people who speak our language or look like us? What if we'd been born outside Y Tir?'

Owain's colour rose. 'That's Emrys Hughes talking, that is. Trust him to stand up for anyone who's "different". We can't save everyone.'

'But we might be able to save more than you and Dad think we can, and we might get more for ourselves into the bargain!'

'Like what?'

'Like heating and medicine…'

'And having computer chips planted in our brains!' Owain interrupted. He was shouting and red-faced now, 'We should save our own country, Alys, and then we can develop the things we want.'

Alys bit her lip and took a deep breath. She spoke quietly, 'Technology is neutral, Owain. It doesn't have to be used against us. We don't have to go back to living in the dark ages to learn from the best parts of the past.'

'I can't believe Dad lets you spend all this time with that Emrys Hughes!' Owain retorted. 'He's rotting your brain. I'll tell you that for nothing. Anyway, I only came up here to say dinner's nearly ready.'

Owain turned and slammed Alys's bedroom door behind him so that the two hundred and fifty year old joists shuddered. Alys sat on the bed and shut her eyes. A picture of Luke sprang to mind, his cool black hair fanning out in a halo around his dark face. Perhaps if she could find another of those trendy art sites to squat, he might find her again. Alys sighed. There were thousands of art sites and what if he did find her site again? What would be the chance of her being online at the same time? She opened her eyes and took in the cold, simple bedroom around her: reality.

Luned

Each night I watch the moon grow. In one life I served the lady of the fountain, leading the man to her, leading him back again when everyone thought he was lost forever.

I have been the shape-shifter in other worlds and now I have made a world for the boy to move through invisibly.

I dreamt about the boy and the magician. They were together again I am the one who will make it happen. I will guide the boy through Annwn. And when he arrives I will be the one waiting.

11

'Back again?' Jodie asked acidly as Luke wandered into the Connexions suite at his school the following Monday morning. Her black hair swung across her face as she bent to wave a hand over the sense screen on her desk. 'You're here to see Billy Morris?' she went on.

Luke stood in front of the sweeping reception desk on its raised plinth feeling small in front of leaf-eyed Jodie, 'Yes.'

Jodie screwed her mouth into a smile, 'That's nice for you. He's waiting in Interview Room three, just down the corridor. Natalie said to remind you that all conversations in the interview rooms are recorded.'

Luke bit his tongue and nodded, 'Right.'

'Well, don't just stand there like someone who's already got an IBS Tag.'

Luke followed the corridor in the direction of Jodie's luminous green-nailed finger and let himself into to Interview Room three. Inside, a thin young man of about twenty was standing by the window, staring out towards the courtyard and Nazir's light fountain sculpture.

The young man turned and nodded at Luke, then turned back to the window, 'Your father did that sculpture, right?'

'Yes.'

'Pretty big-shot name, Nazir Malik.'

'I suppose.'

'Pretty expensive school placement this, isn't it?' He turned to face Luke and Luke took in the bland face: pale, slightly freckled skin and pale grey, almost colourless eyes. 'Live in one of the most expensive pods in the country as well, I hear.'

Luke pushed his hands into the pockets of his perfectly tailored jeans and nodded, feeling ill at ease.

'So, you've got all this luxury and it's not good enough for you, is that it?'

'No. I mean, yes, it's good enough.'

'So what's your problem then?'

Luke gulped. 'I suppose it's just... I mean...' he trailed away.

Billy sat down abruptly and motioned for Luke to do the same in the identical beige chair.

'Okay, so you're a spoiled rich-kid; a Messer who thinks he can mess with the system with no come back. I get that. But I'm here to tell you a few facts, Luke Malik.'

Luke nodded, feeling awkward. He didn't like the way Billy's pale grey eyes stared through him unblinkingly.

'You heard of Serenity Island?'

Luke nodded.

'Know much about it?'

Luke shook his head.

'Not much of a talker for a Messer, are you?'

'Sorry, I, I'm not sure...'

84

'Forget it. Just listen.'

We don't all live in pods like yours, Malik. How many kids in your pod?'

'Twelve.'

'Yeah, all with your own state of the art podroom, no doubt. And how many Guardians?'

'Four.'

'Yeah, well imagine three Guardians to twenty four kids and not like your Guardians either; cretins who couldn't think of anything else to do for a living. Anyway, I shared a podroom with this thug who bullied me since I can remember. Bloody Gary Watlin. So, of course, I quite liked it when I had home visits. Any time away from Gary was all right with me. You get the picture?'

'Yes. Sounds awful. I'd hate to share…'

'Yeah, well spare me your bleeding heart, Malik. I said listen, didn't I?' Billy had a way of curling his thin bottom lip when he asked questions.

Luke retreated back to nodding and hunched down further in his beige chair.

'Right, so I used to pester to get as many home visits as possible and my mother didn't mind me being around, but she wasn't what you'd call a good influence, Malik. Bit like your father, perhaps.'

'No, my father's…'

'I'm not the one you have to convince. Save it for nympho-Natalie in there.'

Luke gulped. He already had suspicions that Natalie had designs on Nazir. Surely she hadn't suggested anything to Billy as well? He was at least ten years younger.

Billy smirked, 'What? Isn't she interested in fifteen year olds or aren't you her type?'

Luke opened his mouth, but closed it again. He took a deep breath, 'You were telling me about your mother.'

'Yeah, I was.'

Billy leant forward in his chair so that his face was only a couple of feet from Luke's, and Luke could smell Billy's breakfast: fats and something sharp and rancid. 'My mother was a bit of a loser. She had these friends in the Subs who filled her head with crap about E-Gov and she filled my head with the same crap.'

Luke felt his eyes widen. His attention was firmly fixed on Billy now, 'So the people in the Subs...'

'I'm not here to tell you about Wasters, Malik, just about what happens if you start to think like them.'

Luke huddled back into his chair. Just a few miles from here, he thought, there could be people living without implants. He wanted to ask Billy a million questions about the Subs and about the people who lived there. How do they live? Do they keep their own children? Instead he forced his attention back to Billy.

'Like I was saying, my Mother filled my head with crap. Why did I have to live in a pod? Why did I have to be forced to go to school? Apparently these Wasters out in the Subs don't even have schools, let alone pods to send their kids to, so I had this mad idea that it would be cool to be like them. Then I stepped up the questions some more. Why couldn't I learn history? You know the score, Malik. All the questions you've been asking. Well, I was way ahead of you, and with a lot more attitude as well. So of course I started getting into trouble. My Guardians stopped my home visits, but that just made me worse. See, the way my bloody mother had messed with my head I thought I was being oppressed. Started bleating on about human rights and all sorts of crap 'cos I couldn't see they were protecting me from her. I didn't do the school work, disrupted lessons, even stood up to bloody Gary Watlin.'

'Good for you,' Luke put in hopefully.

'That's where you're dead wrong, Malik. There are right ways and wrong ways to sort these things out, and that was the wrong way. Heard you got into a scuffle yourself last week?'

'Sort of, but I…'

'Like I said, Malik, not interested, but you're a fool if you go about it the wrong way. Take it from me, E-Gov knows what's what and once you fall into line you realise they were right all along. It's down to you how you learn it, that's all.'

Luke gulped, but kept quiet. He could feel a trickle of cold sweat snaking down his back.

'With me, they tried drugs first. I got a QAD Tag. You know what that is?'

Luke opened his mouth, but Billy answered for him, '"Questioning Authority Disorder." Thing was, I had it bad. The pills took the edge off, but I didn't get better, not really better. So in the end, they sent me to Serenity Island.' Billy made a derisive, snorting noise and raised his palms in a shrug, 'Island! It's a bloody rock with a clapped-out old building and no mod cons, is what it is. But it did the trick, Malik. It does the trick for everyone who's sent there sooner or later.'

Luke sat up straight and waited for Billy to go on. He felt a horrible knotting in this stomach.

Billy stood up and went over to a desk,' Anyway, you can see for yourself. Put these on,' he said, picking up an old fashioned virtual reality visor from the desk.

Luke wondered about the outmoded technology, but decided not to ask questions. He put the visor on and adjusted it to fit. 'I'll fit the ear-piece,' Billy said. Luke tensed as Billy fumbled with the gadget, 'Now just relax and take it all in. This could be your last chance, Malik.'

In the virtual environment, Luke found himself on a beach, a cold-looking sweep of shingle above a strip of weed-covered sand. In front of him was some kind of ancient building, a fortress in grey stone. Luke walked towards the intimidating entrance and into a courtyard. Ahead of him a line of teenagers walked in file behind an older man. There were twelve boys, but not one made a sound other than the steady crunch of boots on gravel. They all wore the same outfit, grey trousers and thick darker grey tops of a material that reminded him of something Alys had worn. What did she call it? Wool? But theirs looked hard and scratchy, not like the soft jumper Alys had worn. The man had on a uniform and carried a short baton. The boys kept their eyes on the ground as they walked and kept an even distance from one another. Luke followed the procession.

'Stop!' The boys halted simultaneously. 'How many times do I have to tell you males to keep your distance?' The uniformed Guardian wandered down the line using his baton to judge distances, roughly pulling boys apart by an extra inch here and there. He's making it up, Luke thought, just looking for an excuse to have a go at them. He hoped Billy had no way of mind-scanning him while he wore this contraption.

The boys reached a room laid out like a class, but with bulky wooden desks instead of sleek screen desks. At the back of the room two large men with longer batons stood unmoving, watching the boys file into rows and take up seats at the desks. At the front of the room, the Guardian, or perhaps he was a Tutor, began a lesson about self esteem, which seemed to consist largely of doing what you were told, as far as Luke could make out. Worse than citizenship lessons, Luke thought grimly. The boys sat stiffly, eyes forward, sometimes nodding slightly. Luke noticed a flicker of movement from one boy, a red-haired, chubby boy of about twelve, who was making small hand gestures mocking the tutor under a table so that the boy next to him had to bite his bottom lip not to smirk.

'Stand, male!' One of the heavies from the back of the class moved to the boy's side, the other was not far behind him. The red haired boy stood up too fast, knocking over his chair so that others around him sucked in their breath and looked away.

'We don't tolerate out of control behaviour in this class, Carey.' The tutor at the front of the class nodded towards the heavies. 'On the ground.'

The red haired boy lay face down on the classroom floor, cold-looking stuff like pavements or stone, Luke noticed, and the heavies leant over him, pulling him into a splayed position, twisting his arms and legs. Luke could see the tears and snot running silently down the boy's face.

'Stay!'

The lesson resumed and the boy stayed on the floor, still as death.

Luke lost track of time, watching the boy, vaguely aware of the monotonous tutor intoning platitudes about emotional growth through obedience.

'Males stand,' the tutor finally commanded. The boys stood and moved mechanically into line, all except the red-haired boy, who was still motionless.

One of the heavies moved towards him, crouched down and twisted an arm painfully behind the boy's back, 'Don't make us have to restrain you again, Carey.'

'No sir, thank you sir.' Carey sniffed.

'Get in line.'

Carey got up stiffly and shuffled into place.

The line followed the tutor to a dining room, dimly lit with a smell that Luke couldn't place, something like an un-flushed toilet he thought for a moment before he noticed the rows of plates steaming on the long refectory tables. Luke wrinkled his nose at the boiled cabbage and fish. It looked grey and unappetizing. In the background a voice track extolled the virtues of healthy eating.

Luke felt Billy at his side and came back to reality with a jolt. With the visor off, he blinked at the light.

'That's how it goes on, Malik. All day every day. You get cold showers and listen to voice tracks to keep you focused. You're never alone. You go to bed at ten. Want to know how you get out?'

Luke nodded. He didn't trust himself to form words.

'When you can convince them that you really believe you deserved to be sent there in the first place, Malik.'

Luke gulped.

'When you can show that you've given up your bad attitudes and said good-bye to your questioning self, when you're really grateful for how they've saved you. Want to know how you go about it?' Billy didn't wait for Luke to nod or gulp, 'You have to get points to get to higher grades.'

'Points?'

'That's what I said, Malik.' Billy moved his face close to Luke so that Luke could smell bad breath again, the same rancid fat smell, but now Luke wondered if the cabbage and fish that smelled like toilets wasn't in the air too. Perhaps that smell stayed around everyone sent to Serenity Island, permanently.

Billy moved back to his chair and sat down heavily.

'I can't see you getting points very fast, either, Malik. You've got too much attitude, like you think you're entitled or something. When you start out at Serenity Island you are nothing, absolutely nothing. You have to learn that before you can move on. Nothing is exactly what it says – nothings don't talk, don't stand unless they're told to, don't move without permission. You are nothing. When you get it, when you start to act like a nothing then you might start to get some points. Every ten points is a new level, but it's like that kids' game, Malik, you can go down the snakes if you blow it, back to nothing again. When you have forty points you can choose your own clothes, within reason of course. Once you get to sixty points you join the heavies three days a week. You get to rat out the lower down kids, discipline them, give them forfeits or take their points off them and of course you're watched like a hawk. Any leniency you show is held against you. Get the picture?'

'Yes,' Luke's voice came out strangled and Billy grinned.

'So you see, it's all up to you, Malik. No one forces you to do anything, but if you don't, well... you've only got yourself to blame, see?'

Luke nodded again.

'Well, I hope you do, Malik. Go back into the programme. I've got another bit I want you to see.'

Luke obeyed and found himself back in the grey fortress of Serenity Island, standing outside a small room. The room, more like a large shower cubicle, was tiled white, though the tiles were dirty and marked, many of them cracked. On the tiled floor a girl lay on her face, arms by her sides, so still that for a moment Luke wondered if she were dead. Two women stood over her, unflinching, the same cold, slightly sneering expressions on their faces that Luke noticed earlier on the male heavies in the classroom.

Luke watched, appalled.

'Stretch time, female,' one of the bulky sneering women said after a while.

The girl moved slowly, wincing with pain. She faltered when she stood up and almost fell, but the women either side didn't make a move to help her. Luke stretched out a useless virtual hand and then remembered that Billy would be watching him. The girl, about fifteen and with long mousy hair that looked like it had once been well-cut, but now was stringy and unkempt, made some cautious stretching movements and bit down hard on her lip.

'Okay, that's enough limbering. You're not a ballet dancer here, female, you're nothing. Back on the floor.'

The girl lowered herself slowly, biting her lip harder, but she glanced up before she lay flat, tears welling in her pale brown eyes, 'I... I...' she hesitated, fighting back to the sobs.

'Did you hear a noise?' one of the women asked, sneering harder.

'Couldn't have been nothing talking, could it?' The other one joined in. She edged a foot over to the girl on the floor, poking her with the toe of her boot, as though she had found some unknown flotsam on the scummy beach outside. 'Nothing doesn't make a noise, surely?'

The girl whimpered and lowered her head, but the first guard was over her, a boot on either side of her thin body. The woman crouched, forced a heavy hand into the small of the girl's back and pressed hard. 'You know the position, female and you will learn to want to obey. That's an extra day in here for you,' she shoved hard again, 'which means, of course, you've got another night sleeping out in the corridor.'

The woman stepped back from the girl, who was as still and quiet as death again. Luke glanced down the corridor. At one end it was open to the elements and there was a cold, constant wind moaning along it. At the other end Luke noticed a mattress, a thin roll of grey, scratchy looking fabric no more than a few millimetres thick and a darker grey blanket, wool again, but as harsh looking as a pan scourer.

Luke felt Billy at his elbow and removed the visor. He let out a long sigh. He was feeling dizzy now and desperate to get away from Billy, but he kept his face as impassive as he could manage.

Billy sat down. 'When kids go in, Malik, they're full of themselves. We deserve what we get. You go on being disrespectful and you'll only have yourself to blame. And if it happens, Malik, you've got to reckon you need to do the work. It's only for your own good.'

Luke listened to Billy and shivered. He understood suddenly what it was about Billy that was so unsettling; not the bad breath, but the emptiness. Billy's tone was almost robotic, his eyes empty of emotion except an occasional sneer, no doubt picked up when he took his turn to stand over kids lower down the pecking order.

'I could show you a circle-sharing if you want to see more.' Billy said, cutting across Luke's thoughts.

Luke hesitated. He wanted to leave, but he was anxious not to appear disinterested or Billy might say something dire to Natalie. 'What's that exactly?' he blustered.

'Each cell group has a time once a week when the kids have to share how they're doing, what's bothering them, that kind of thing. You can't have secrets from your cell.'

'But how do they know the kids are telling the truth?'

'They know. Your Guardians are on to you 24-7. What are you thinking? Why aren't you thinking about this improvement? What are you thinking now? They don't need mind calling implants in there. When it's sharing time people know if you're faking or holding back and everyone chips in to help you get over any bad attitude. No one pulls their punches. If you can't take it or you hold back you lose points or your Guardian might send you straight to TT if he asks you to spill something private and you don't spill.'

'TT?'

'Thinking Time. Like that girl you just saw. In TT you have uninterrupted time to get your mind with the programme.'

'So people tell on themselves?'

'Of course. Why not? You're there to improve, Malik, not to go on with your old bad ways.'

'And what happens when you've told on yourself?'

'Depends what it is. A couple of revelations get picked out most weeks for the communal dinner on Fridays. The kid stands there while his Guardian tells, then anyone can speak, even the nothings, as long as it's to take a turn ripping into the kid's bad attitude. You can really pick up some points if you make some good remarks against the kid in trouble.'

Luke swallowed and shifted uneasily in his chair.

'Want to see?' Billy sounded bored now, but Luke wasn't taking any chances.

'Thanks,' Luke said co-operatively.

Circle-sharing was as chilling as Luke had imagined. The red haired boy, Carey, stood and cried for about ten minutes after confessing to a bad thought about a girl in another cell. The other kids shot spiteful remarks at him until he became almost hysterical with tears, and the sneering Guardian in charge sent for a heavy to take Carey to TT to think about his self-indulgent whining.

Luke handed the visor back to Billy with his stomach churning.

'So what's it going to be, Malik?' Luke looked at the floor, searching for an answer. 'You'd better decide quick. Get your act together or it's Serenity Island.'

'I'll get my act together,' Luke said, mentally kicking himself for not being able to muster more than a mumbled reply out of his tight, dried up throat.

'Yeah, well. That's not for me to say. Jodie'll make you an appointment to see Natalie next week She'll know what to do with you for the best.'

Myrddin Emrys

It has always been this way for Artur. I cannot be with him in the battle. It is not the way of Druids and bards to take up the sword, but I will be in his head and heart. In one life I tasted his fear as he faced his enemies, at Badon and at Camlan where he was betrayed and cut down. In this life I have watched over him from my glass tower. I whispered stories over him when he was young; stories that will be his own soon, very soon.

12

Luke stood in the school courtyard trembling. He told himself it was cold, there was snow in the air, but he could feel his clothes reacting to the air temperature to warm him. This chill had nothing to do with the weather. Everyone would be out of class in ten minutes, queuing for dinner, Bradley and his cronies would, no doubt, be eager to ask him sarcastic questions about his meeting with Billy. Luke needed to be somewhere else, but where and how? The tags in his clothes would trigger as soon as he walked anywhere, not to mention his implant, which would soon alert the school to his whereabouts if he was missed, and of course he would be missed.

Luke hesitated, and then psyched himself up to act. He had to have time to think, he told himself. He stalked towards the administrator's office.

'Good afternoon, Luke Malik,' a mechanical voice intoned as Luke went through the office door.

The secretary behind the office desk smiled at Luke. She was a middle aged woman with a moon-like face, freckles and blue eyes that Luke noted were her own, not lenses like Jodie's.

'Hello, Luke, how can I help you?'

Luke smiled back. Don't act paranoid, he told himself. 'Er, it's a bit of favour actually.' He put on his most winning grin.

'I see,' the secretary, whose name display read 'Louise Hillier' smiled back, waiting for Luke to go on.

'It's just my father has this big Winterval art launch coming up and there's a pre-launch reception tomorrow night and I totally forgot to get a card or anything. I wondered if I could get a town pass for lunch break and period three. I've got a study slot in period three, and I could make it up at the pod tonight.' Luke tried not to talk too fast, not to seem too desperate.

'We...ll.' Louise flicked the screen on her desk momentarily, 'Go on, then.'

Luke almost skipped in the air, 'Thanks. That's great. Really. Thanks!'

Louise entered something onto the screen. 'There you go, Luke, you're all clear. You make sure you're back for period four mind.'

'Yes,' Luke agreed, feeling guilty about the trouble Louise might be in later.

Outside the school grounds Luke hesitated. The Bullring was full of purposeful people going to the smartest shops or cafés or entering the security vestibules of the premier offices in the city. He could walk to Nazir's house in ten minutes, past Victoria Square and out along the canal where the most exclusive apartments and occasional houses nestled in the richest part of the city, but what could Nazir do but return him to school, and then what? Luke could feel his skin turning clammy despite the smart material of his t-shirt. He put his head down, hunched his shoulders and walked to the nearest credit point. He inserted his card, regretting the expensive hair style. The number that flashed on the screen made Luke smile genuinely for the first time that day. Nazir must have topped up his credit. Relieved, Luke withdrew the card and headed for the monorail station. So far surveillance would have picked him up doing permitted things, but once he headed out of the city, how long would it be before his transmitters alerted a response? Luke paused. He couldn't simply get on the monorail. Now what? Luke stood still in the crowded street, almost tripping a fast moving, suited woman who scowled and muttered something in his direction.

Luke headed into the nearest mall and made his way to a large chemist's shop.

'Welcome, Luke Malik. We hope you enjoy shopping with us today,' a mechanical voice purred as the shop doors opened for him.

Luke headed for the first aid counter. He picked up a pack of large plasters, the kind with coagulant and sterile properties and paid at the automatic till, feeding the plasters and then his card along the checkout. Outside he found a lift and headed towards a modelling shop he had visited with his father.

'Thank you for choosing Midland Modelling for your art and creative supplies. We hope we can find the right product for you today, Luke,' the door voice said cheerily.

Luke found an assistant at the tools counter, 'Er, I need a modelling knife, like a Stanley knife or something, something with a sharp blade.'

'Right, well we have a range of …'

Luke blinked. He realised he hadn't heard anything the smiling assistant had said to him. 'Er, just a basic one's fine, as long as the blade's good.' Luke caught the slight look of concern on the assistant's face. 'I'm doing some modelling with my father.'

The assistant glanced down at his counter screen and resumed his fixed, placid smile, 'Ah, Nazir Malik. It must be an honour to learn from such a great artist. Perhaps this one…'

'Yeah, that's fine.'

Outside, Luke glanced at his watch. He had two and a half hours until the alarm would be raised and he'd already used half an hour. He realised suddenly that he was hungry. Claudia had been unable to persuade him to have breakfast this morning while the interview with Billy had been hanging over him. If he didn't eat now, it could be a long time until the next meal. Luke ducked back into the mall and caught the lift to the dining mezzanine. He ate fast, hardly tasting the chicken and mayonnaise oozing out of his baguette. He swilled down orange juice and a sudden thought of his mother among her orange trees sprang to mind. Luke blinked back a tear. Lunch over, he headed for monorail.

He bought his ticket, ignoring the screen voice blurting his name to anyone who cared to hear, and got on board the first monorail going in the right direction.

Once in the carriage, Luke headed for the toilet cubicle, grateful that the automated door didn't sing out his name or wish him a successful visit to the facilities. He had fifteen minutes before reaching the Subs, a place called Telford that had only ever been a scary story to Luke. He would have to lose his tracking device before the monorail left the Connected Zone, the poorer margins of the city where the service workers lived, but where surveillance and connection were still high. For a second, Luke contemplated mind-calling Kyle, one last call before he was cut off, for how long? Perhaps for ever, but he steeled himself and dismissed the thought. He would only cause his friend trouble if he called.

Luke laid a plaster out on the tiny counter by the basin, took off his jacket, t-shirt and scarf and let them fall in a scrunched heap on the spotless floor of the cubicle. He sat down on the toilet seat and reached into his back pocket for the blade. Luke carefully unwound the wrapping and took a deep breath. He put the blade next to the plaster and reached both hands round to the back of his neck. He could feel the tiny connection coil on his neck to the left of his spine. He kept his left hand on the spot and picked up the blade with his right. He placed the blade over the hard lump that the coil made on his skin and breathed deeply again, steadying his hand. On the next breath he pressed hard, wincing with pain. He pressed again and felt a wave of queasiness. With his left hand he eased the coil out and let the knife drop.

Luke reached quickly for paper towels to staunch the blood, and then fumbled the plaster into position. The first one wrinkled and folded in on itself and Luke had to unwrap a second, which he managed to secure into place. He felt the sterile coagulant gel cooling the stinging wound. He dampened more paper towels to make sure there were no traces of blood left on him, then put on his t-shirt and jacket, carefully folding the winter scarf around the place where the plaster would be visible between his hairline and t-shirt.

He felt uncomfortable still, but the coil was out. Luke picked up the tiny transmitter, tipped it into the toilet bowl and flushed. It bobbed back on the surface of the water, but on the third flush it finally vanished from sight. Luke went back into the monorail carriage and sank into an empty chair. The carriage was almost empty now, as they moved further towards the Subs. Luke glanced at his watch, the fifteen minute journey was nearly over.

Further down the carriage he heard a sharp metallic ring and watched a middle aged woman rummage in a dog-eared handbag for a mobile phone, the kind used by people without mind-call enhancement.

'I'm nearly home, darling. Five minutes,' the woman assured the tiny hand-set.

Luke had the sudden feeling of being slapped as the magnitude of what he had done hit him. He had left the world he knew behind, there would be no more mind-calling and he didn't even own a mobile. Even if he did, it would only make him traceable. He had cut himself off, literally. The train pulled into a station and the middle aged woman deferentially moved aside for him as they reached the door together. He still looked like one of the connected, he realised, but that was all he had now, the appearance of being someone.

On the platform, Luke hesitated. A monorail guard eyed him warily and Luke felt suddenly exposed. No-one in the Subs would have a hair style like this, none of them would be wearing clothes made from smart materials. Even his jeans and t-shirt stood out, but there was no going back. Luke followed the arrows to the monorail exit, shocked by how different everything was. There was litter on the floor and the corridor leading to the exit was grubby and smelled like the cabbage and fish from the virtual visit to Serenity Island, only this time it was real. Luke wrinkled his nose in disgust and tried not to retch.

He emerged onto a street of grey houses, interspersed with occasional run-down shops, unlike anything Luke had ever seen. Between the buildings were stretches of waste land from which square, high rise buildings rose, nothing like the sleek modern office buildings or carefully restored apartments of the city.

A gang of youths slouched in a group a few yards away. One of them spat in Luke's direction.

'Hey, little Beaut-lost! Fuck off back to yow're own world if yow know what's good for yow.'

Luke put his head down and slunk along the street in the opposite direction. He could hear the jibes and insults continuing as he walked, but the gang didn't follow him. He turned down the first side street and paused, leaning heavily against a wall made of large grey blocks. 'Great plan, Luke! Now what?' he said out loud. Despite his clothing he could feel the bite of the December air on his face and his hands were bitterly cold. He pushed them into his pockets and slouched against a wall. He took a deep breath and looked up for a street sign. Summer Place, the dull metallic sign read. Luke steadied himself. Good, he knew where he was, he should keep track. He closed his eyes to enter his home page. He would call up a map of the area, keep track. He opened his eyes feeling dizzy.

'You're not connected, idiot!' he said out loud to the icy air.

He kept walking and sifted through his brain. Without connection, without enhanced memory, so much was missing. Luke thought this must be what it was like for someone to lose an arm or leg, the sensation of some part of himself simply gone, but still almost there, just beyond reach. He staggered as he walked. He needed to sit down. At the end of the street was a corner café, a dingy, uninviting place with chipped melamine counters that looked like something out of a movie set from one of the retro-films he'd downloaded illicitly with Kyle. Luke pushed the door open and stood still as every eye in the café turned towards him.

'Yow coming or going?' The man behind the counter was as sharp and thin as his voice, 'We 'aven't all got brainy clothes to warm us up, Beaut. Yow're letting the soddin' winter in.'

Luke took a step forward and let the door swing closed behind him. He tried not to notice the shabbily dressed, staring people as he approached the counter.

'I'd like a hot chocolate, please.' Luke said, steadying his voice carefully.

'Would yow really? Well I'd like to see yer money, Beaut.'

Luke thought of telling the man that he was not a Beaut, but thought better of it. Instead he fumbled in his jacket pocket, brought out his wallet and pulled his card from it, offering it the man, who now stood with his arms folded, a nasty-looking grin on his thin face.

Thin Face spoke slowly, as though explaining to an idiot. 'I said money, Beaut. That's a card, a lump of plastic that is of no use to yow here, so yow can flash it all yow like. No money, no chocolate.'

Luke stuffed his card back into his pocket without bothering to put it in the wallet. 'Right, sorry. Is there a credit point round here?' his voice was wavering now.

'Turn right, second block along. Watch out for the bad boys,' Thin Face added scathingly.

Luke scuttled back to the café door, trying not to hear the muttered insults from the tables he passed. He stood for a moment in front of the door, confused that it wasn't opening for him, then remembered that he would have to open it himself.

In the street he caught his breath. He could feel the redness of his face and his heart was pounding too fast.

He turned right and headed in the direction of the credit point. He had never seen real money before, let alone withdrawn it, but in theory his card should work, provided the disappearance of his tracking device somewhere on the edge of the Connected Zone hadn't triggered an alert yet. Behind him, Luke could hear footsteps, but it was best not to glance back, he thought.

He reached the machine and put in his card, his hand shaking so that it took two attempts. The machine made beeping noises and flashed messages on a screen, but didn't speak to him. Luke sighed with relief; his credit hadn't been blocked yet. He hastily withdrew everything and shoved the strange notes into his wallet. The footsteps behind him got closer and Luke turned to face a circle of five youths, faces he had noticed huddled round one of the tables at the café.

Luke froze. 'So yow got yer money, then, Beaut?' The youth who spoke had long, lank hair and acne so bad that it resembled a relief map.

Luke nodded, feeling stupid. He could feel tears pressing behind his eyes, but he wouldn't cry.

'Good, an' seeing as 'ow yow're on our turf, yow won't mind 'anding it over to us, will yow?' Luke stood, mesmerised, it was all he could do to decipher the words through the strange accent. Confusion and fear rooted him to the spot.

'Am yow listenin'?' Another youth demanded, a fat, lard-white boy with skin like wet paper pulp.

Luke nodded, but still didn't move.

'Think the Beauts goin' to wet itself soon,' Acne Face smirked. 'Yow're all right, Beaut, yow jus' give us the money, then we'll let yow piss off back to where yow belong.'

Luke wondered briefly about the Stanley knife, but there were five boys and maybe they had knives too. He pushed his hand into his pocket to reach for the money, perhaps he could fish out only a part of it without them realising.

From behind the gang another voice spoke up, 'Okay, Sheldon, you've had your fun. You'd better back off now.'

The gang rounded on the voice, a tall, thin boy a couple of years older than Luke with the palest skin, hair and eyes Luke had ever seen. Behind him a girl of the same age hovered uneasily. She had skin a shade darker than Luke's and hair almost to her thighs that seemed to be knotted into frayed ropes.

'Am yow gonna make me back off, Zach Hindmarsh, or what?' Acne Face demanded unpleasantly.

'No, the Regs will make you back off, Sheldon,' the pale boy said wearily, 'about thirty seconds after he makes a mind call for help. Look at him, you idiot. You don't even need to touch him, all you have to do is scare him enough and he mind calls for help and your life's finished, you moron. And the rest of us will have the Regs crawling all over our sorry lives for weeks.'

Sheldon's gang began to edge backwards, muttering. Sheldon tensed, but then shrugged his shoulders and grinned. 'No 'arm done, Beaut, eh? Yow can take a bit of laugh, can't yow?'

Luke nodded.

'There ya, then, like I said. Just a laugh. We'll be off, eh, lads? Yow enjoy yow chocolate now.'

Sheldon and his gang sauntered away, each aping the same casual gait, slapping one another on the back and laughing as they went.

'Morons!' Zach shot after them. He turned towards Luke. 'Well, er, you'll probably be wanting to get on your way. If you need directions to the monorail station…'

The girl sidled up to Zach, 'It gets dark early at this time of year,' she added nervously, 'someone might come looking for you.'

Luke sighed. Out here he spelled trouble to everyone. How could he have imagined he'd find anything other than hostility or fear in the Subs? He stepped slowly towards the couple.

'Thanks for helping just then.'

'Yeah, well, better for me to talk some sense into them than for the Regs to swoop down on them and anyone else that gets in their way.'

Luke took a deep breath, 'You don't need to worry. The Regs won't be swooping. I can't call.'

Zach and the girl look confused.

'I'm kind of on the run. I took my PTI out with a modelling knife.'

'Shit!' Zach responded, 'You mean you're out here looking like that with no connection and your credit about to be cut off any second?'

Luke nodded, 'The credit card doesn't matter, though. I emptied it.'

Zach whistled and rolled his eyes, 'And I thought they were morons!'

Luke looked down at the dirty pavement.

'You'd better come back to our place,' he heard the girl say.

'Saskia!' Zach swung round, aghast.

'We can't just leave him, Zach. He'll be dead before tomorrow morning.'

Zach turned back to Luke, 'Are you sure no-one can trace you, Beaut?' he demanded roughly.

'Positive. I got my tracker out before I reached the Subs, and flushed it. They'll know I'm missing and which monorail I got on, but not where I got off. I'm off the surveillance system.'

'Yeah, well, I suppose you've at least widened the search area, Beaut.'

'I'm not a Beaut, by the way,' Luke ventured.

'Yeah? What do you call that?' Zach asked, pointing to the halo of black hair hovering stylishly above Luke's head.

Luke grinned. 'A mistake. I did it to impress a girl, but it didn't work.'

'Is that why you're running?' Saskia asked. She had a quiet voice, Luke thought, nervous and child-like.

'No, nothing like that. I was in a bit of trouble. I was in danger of being shipped off to a place called Serenity Island where they re-form you. I just had to get away.'

Zach nodded, 'Sounds pretty heavy, mate. Okay, so you'd better come with us. At least it'll give you time to think about things instead of panicking your way out of a crisis.' Zach smiled for the first time, 'Got to hand it to you for guts, mate.'

'Thanks. I can pay you something for...'

'You keep your money, mate, you're probably going to need it more than me, by the sounds of things I'm Zach, by the way and this is Saskia, my girlfriend,' Zach emphasised the 'my'. 'And you are?'

'Luke Malik.'

'Ha! Malik, same name as that big-shot artist.'

Luke nodded, 'Yeah, he's my father...' Luke said before wondering whether he would have been better to keep quiet about that.

'No shit! They really aren't going to be happy about losing you, are they?' Luke grinned and shrugged. 'Come on then, We'd better get you off the streets.'

Nazir

It has begun. Denver Horace and his team of officious Regulators found nothing and left assuring me that they wouldn't allow my good name to be tainted by the boy. They are anxious that I go ahead with the Winterval opening, that everything should appear to be normal. Fools. They did not for a moment suspect that they were speaking to my virtual self.

It is time for me to weave more illusions. In one life I made Wthyr appear as Ygraine's husband, not to serve Wthyr's lust, but so that Artur would be born. In this life I'm the one with two identities and sometimes the power of illusion is needed so that I can be in two places at once

It is hard to leave behind Vivian's garden and my glass tower. In one life it was my prison, but in this life it has been my sanctuary. The installation waits there now, ready to be moved to the unveiling.

13

Alys juddered awake suddenly. The familiar cold air of her room wrapped around her. It had snowed on and off for almost a week now, but after the first heavy fall, that had kept her mother at home for a day, the snow had turned wet and slushy and hadn't lain thickly. It was still night, but around the edge of one curtain Alys could see the faint white haze that marked a deeper snowfall. She sat up feeling anxious, as though there was something urgent that she had forgotten to do. Something teased at the corner of her mind, light as a bird's foot print in snow. What was it? Alys got up and shivered. She pulled on her thick dressing gown and wrapped her favourite red carthen round her shoulders. Hunched onto the broad slate slab of her low windowsill, she watched the swollen tongue of the river frothing beyond Taid's poly-tunnels, a lick of black against the ghostly white world. She closed her eyes and tried to piece together the fading dream images, but they were beyond her grasp. She shook herself and rubbed her arms, the encryption – it was something to do with the encryption, but what?

She couldn't capture the lost fragments of thought and was too wide awake now to go back to bed. 4 a.m. Alys crept downstairs. She would make hot chocolate and sit at her computer, perhaps something would come back to her. Downstairs, the kitchen light was already on. It wasn't like her dad to forget to turn out a light when he went to bed. Alys pushed the door open gently. Taid was dozing in the armchair by the wood-burning stove. His eyes flickered open as Alys entered.

'Are you all right, Taid?'

Tomas pulled himself stiffly upright and forced a smile, 'Fine, Alys, cariad. You don't need much sleep when you get to my age.' Tomas stretched and Alys noticed the same wincing movement that he'd made at breakfast a couple of days ago, 'but what about you? Bit early for you to be up, isn't it?'

'I had a weird dream, Taid. I think I realised something about the encryption, but then I woke up I couldn't remember it. You know that feeling when something you've dreamt is really vivid, but you still can't recall it properly?'

Tomas nodded, 'Just like Gwen you are. You should go back to bed.'

'I won't sleep now, Taid. I thought I'd make some hot chocolate…'

'And sit at your computer with it, worrying away at the problem,' Tomas said, smiling.

Alys returned the grin, 'Yes. I'm so close, Taid, I know there's something I've almost worked out. Can I make anything for you?'

Tomas shook his head, 'Don't you fret about me. I'm fine in my chair here. I'll get some tea in a bit.'

Alys bit her lip, but didn't argue.

Upstairs, she pored over the encrypted passwords, entered formulae that she had tried before, walked around her room to keep warm and then started again and again. 7 a.m. She went down to breakfast to find Taid and Gwen sitting opposite one another drinking tea and talking in almost whispers.

Gwen startled as Alys entered and got up quickly, 'Alys, cariad, we're all early birds today. I'll get you some breakfast.' Gwen bustled towards the fridge and began setting eggs by the range.

Alys looked out at the snow, 'Is it too deep to get over to Emrys's, Mam?'

Gwen eyed the crisp white blankness outside the window, 'Could be, cariad, but I need to take more morphine over to Beddgelert, so I could drop you off. We'll just have to hope we can make it back, that's all.'

'Thanks, Mam,' Alys said, pouring out a mug of steaming tea, 'I have this half idea that I can't shake off and I'd like to talk to Emrys about it. It's not the same on email. We need to bounce ideas off each other.'

Owain stood at the kitchen door glowering, 'You're going over to Emrys Hughes' in this weather? You want your head examined.'

'Morning, Owain,' Gwen put in a little too cheerfully, 'Ready for a nice bit of breakfast, cariad?'

'Could do with a bit of help in the tunnel today, Owain,' Tomas added, doing his bit to change the subject.

Owain scowled and scraped back a kitchen chair. Alys poured more tea and slid a mug over to him.

'Dad, you don't think Alys should be going off to Emrys Hughes' place in this snow, do you?' Owain persisted as Geraint entered the kitchen.

'Is it urgent, Alys?' Geraint asked. He stood by the window squinting into the snow-laden sky, 'Could get really heavy before the day's out and I don't want you stuck over there.'

'Yes,' Alys said stubbornly, 'if I don't see Emrys today I might lose this idea. I'm only just clinging on to a shadow of it, as it is. And Mam can drop me on her way to Beddgelert. I don't need to stay long.'

Geraint sighed and nodded. Gwen put plates on the table and Owain hunched over his food, jabbing at it testily.

'Well, did it help?' Gwen asked later when she collected Alys on the return journey from Beddgelert.

Alys bit her lip, 'Maybe. I've got some more ideas at least. I think I'll have to sleep on it though. I'm going to put a flash light and paper by my bed tonight, make sure I don't lose the ideas if I have another dream.'

Gwen smiled and nodded, 'I used to dream answers to assignments when I was a medical student,' she offered, 'And sometimes I still dream what it is that's wrong with someone or what it is that needs to be done for them.'

Alys smiled. 'How is Nain Parry?'

Gwen shook her head slowly, 'Not long now, Alys, but she's as comfortable as can be. I suppose we should be grateful she's gone on this long. She was Nain to

117

everyone when I was a child and she could give Tomas twenty years, but it's like an institution passing away. All those memories,' Gwen trailed away.

'Mam,' Alys took a deep breath, 'Mam, is Taid ill?'

Gwen slowed down involuntarily and shot Alys a quick, anxious glance, 'Yes, cariad.'

'Is he..? Is he going to..?'

'I think so, cariad, yes.' Gwen said quietly.

Alys choked back a tear, 'What… what is it?'

'Cancer, cariad. His liver. He won't take the chemotherapy, though.'

'In E-Gov they could cure that, right?'

Gwen nodded, 'The new genetic modifications on the richer children mean they'll never get it in the first place, Alys, but there are injections for lots of cancers, too.'

'We'll crack the encryption, Mam, I know we will.'

They drove back to Tŷ Meirion in silence.

At home, Alys picked at her dinner. She noticed how Gwen put less on Tomas' plate, obviously an agreement they had made, and how Taid still left food uneaten. Geraint and Owain were in bullish mood, full of bluster about Dewi Jenkins, who would be in Brussels by now.

'You better remember these dates, Alys,' Owain said. He was smiling, but belligerent, Alys thought, hoping for her to take the bait. 'Tuesday December 19th 2075, the day Y Tir began negotiations to become a Free State and Wednesday 20th December, the day we finally got independence. That'll make the Solstice something to celebrate.'

Alys shot Owain half a smile, but didn't reply. She took another spoon of lamb cawl and looked busy with her food.

'How's Nain Parry?' Tomas asked quietly.

Gwen set her spoon down and brushed back a stray strand of red-gold hair that was salted with tobacco-grey, 'As comfortable as I can make her, Tomas. It won't be long now.'

Tomas nodded, 'Now that's a date to remember, Owain lad, the end of an era. 1983 Nain Parry was born. Her son Liam was only three years younger than me, died not long after my Megan, caught pneumonia living in the mines when we went underground. It'll be a real loss when Nain Parry goes.' Tomas brushed a hand across his eye and Alys began to reach out to him, but then pulled back. Dad and Owain didn't know that Taid was ill and he wouldn't thank her for giving him away before he was ready.

'Once we're independent, Taid, there'll be no need for skulking in mines or anywhere else,' Owain said a little too loudly.

'Ah well, now,' Tomas countered gently, 'freedom's never forever, mind. You have to watch out for it. Tyranny's only ever a stone's throw away, and it doesn't always come in the guises we expect.'

'We'll watch out for it all right, Taid,' Owain said emphatically, 'Y Tir will go from strength to strength.

By the time you're Nain Parry's age you won't recognise the place.'

Alys saw her mother duck her head, then scrape back her chair and begin clattering away dishes.

'I'll get those, Mam,' Alys offered eager to be away from the kitchen table too.

Out of sight of the boys, by the sink, Alys quickly grabbed Gwen and hugged her hard. Gwen nodded and smiled, then went back to the table to collect more dishes, 'You start loading the dishwasher, Alys,' Gwen called over her shoulder, 'Owain, why don't you put on a kettle for me?'

'Lovely cawl, Gwen,' Geraint said, 'You should sit down and let others do the clearing up now. You look a bit tired.'

'I'm fine,' Gwen insisted, 'absolutely fine.' She forced a smile and continued to bustle.

'I'm a bit tired myself,' Tomas put in, 'Think I'll get an early night tonight.'

Geraint shot his father a puzzled glance, 'You all right, Dad?'

'I'm fine, just a bit of a long day. Bit of cold in my bones, that's all.'

'Shall I bring you some tea, Taid?' Alys asked.

'Thank you, cariad, that'd be just the job.'

Geraint stood looking after his father as he made his way along the corridor and upstairs. He waited for him to begin ascending the second set of stairs, out of ear-shot and turned towards his wife, 'Did Dad leave some food tonight, Gwen?'

'Just a bit,' Gwen said without turning to face her husband.

Geraint shook his head. 'Not like him. Hope he's not coming down with something.'

Alys filled Taid's favourite mug with tea and scuttled out of the kitchen. Upstairs she knocked on the door across the landing from her own and stepped into Taid's long room with thin windows at both ends and another on the third wall, looking towards the Ffestiniog valley. Taid sat in his armchair fingering a book of photos.

'Can I see, Taid?'

Tomas handed Alys the album in exchange for the steaming mug of tea.

'Gwen told you then?' he said simply.

Alys nodded, 'I kind of guessed, Taid,' she choked on her words and sat down on the edge of Taid's bed.

'You're not to fret, cariad. It's my time that's all.'

Alys nodded, unconvinced, and then forced a smile, 'Tell me about King Arthur, Taid. I want my Artur page to be perfect.'

Tomas took a deep gulp of tea and settled back into his chair, 'Pass that carthen then, cariad,' Alys tucked the red and blue blanket around Tomas in his chair and settled onto his neatly made bed.

'There's comfy,' Tomas smiled, before beginning in the way he always did, 'There are so many stories about Artur…'

Alys closed her eyes and let her grandfather's musical voice drift over her, only opening them when

121

she heard a catch in his breath. Tomas shifted his dwindling weight in the chair and Alys saw him wince.

She bit her lip, 'Are you all right to go on, Taid?'

'I'm fine, cariad, fine, unless you're itching to get to your computer.'

'No. I want to listen.'

Tomas nodded and took up his story where he had left off. 'It was obvious to Artur's company that he was the only worthy successor to Ambrosius… In the end it wasn't a matter for debate. After a victory against all the odds the men wouldn't rest till he was crowned so Merddin crowned him on a hill in southern England, on the eye of an ancient chalk horse carved into the downs by another ancient people.'

'Have you ever been there, Taid?'

Tomas nodded, 'When I was a child, but I can still remember it.' He reached for a piece of paper from a pile of books and papers on a rickety old oak table beside his chair and sketched three or four curving lines, the suggestion of a galloping horse.

'It looks so modern, Taid, so simple.'

Tomas nodded again, 'It does Alys, simple and beautiful it is. The White Horse of Uffington.'

'But the Saxons didn't leave, Taid?' Alys had heard the answer a thousand times, but she wanted Tomas to go on. She wanted his voice to be ingrained in her mind for ever.

'No, cariad. They made a bargain with Artur. It wasn't such a stupid thing, with all that coastline to defend and whole countries of Saxons waiting to be next to try their luck. The Saxons who'd already settled here agreed to stop new invaders from flooding in. Artur had trouble on all sides and he was only one man. Even a couple of the princes of Cymru whispered that Artur should forget his Roman sword and the rest of Britain and only look after his own people.' Tomas grinned suddenly and Alys thought he looked ten years younger for a moment, as mischievous as Owain when he wanted to tease, 'There are always some of us who want to keep freedom and goodness a close secret, Alys.'

Alys grinned back. Tomas had refused to be drawn into the growing family feud over the best future for The Standing Ground, but Alys felt suddenly reassured that her grandfather could see further than Geraint and Owain.

'After a failed harvest, the Scots invaded Môn and the coast of Gwynedd,' Tomas continued, 'Artur camped at Caernarfon and fought the Scots back, but the next fight was already waiting and he knew he'd never see home again... It was a time of betrayals: Medraut, two Welsh princes, others making new alliances. It was the same story when E-Gov snuck up on us, Alys. People who we counted on let us down.' Tomas shifted and winced before continuing, 'Cerdic and Merdaut put out a call to the Scots and the Picts of Gaul and soon massed an army and, to make things worse, it was harvest time again...

'When death came, Artur's sword was thrown into the lake as a signal to Constantine. Bedwyr kept Artur's death secret until the fighting ended and never told anyone where the grave was. To this day we don't know where Artur is buried, but the legend persists that in our greatest time of need he will return.'

Alys sat up. 'And will he, Taid?'

'Perhaps he already has, cariad. Perhaps he returns every time people stand their ground.'

Tomas looked suddenly deflated and Alys stood and kissed her grandfather good-night. The skin of his forehead was like dry paper and he looked pale, perhaps with a tinge of sallow yellow, though perhaps it was only the evening light coming off the snow, Alys tried to reassure herself.

In her bedroom Alys sat gazing out of the window for a long time, looking at the lights of Tanygrisiau shining through the darkness. She wondered what Luke was doing at this moment.

Myrddin Emrys

For now he is safe. In one lifetime Cei stood with him to the end and Bedwyr was there to carry out his last wish, even Gwenhwyfar returned at the end. In this lifetime there are allies as well as those who lay in wait.

As he makes his journey Luned's dreams will become more powerful. She is close to cracking the code. She begins to know who she is and to sense the strength of her powers, her maths and her magic. The boy will not be able to enter her virtual worlds that are more real than his artificial pod-life, but she will find a way to him. She is the guide, she always finds the way.

14

Zach turned towards a tower block that stood across the street from the credit point and Luke followed him. The vestibule smelled like the monorail station, urine and something else, something sour and noxious. Zach shot a wry smile in Luke's direction, 'Piss and vomit, mate, in case you're wondering.'

Luke made a face.

'You get used to it. Just don't try taking the lifts. The smell's too much in there and anyway the lifts are dangerous places, strictly drug deals and quickies.'

Luke nodded and tried not to look too shocked, but he could feel his colour rising. He followed Zach and Saskia up flight after flight of stairs, losing count of which landing they were on.

'Welcome to our home,' Zach grinned as he unlocked a door like a metal cage. Inside he unlocked two bolts and finally turned the door key, 'Sorry about the slow entrance, mate.'

Inside the flat, Luke followed the couple down a narrow corridor. The walls on either side were painted a warm orange colour over paper that was peeling away around the brown skirting boards. They passed a door on either side then came to a door at the end of the corridor. The room beyond was long and thin, a living room at one end and a kitchen at the other, so primitive that Luke couldn't hazard a guess as to what some of the gadgets might do. He felt increasingly disoriented, as though he'd stepped onto another planet. On the battered resin table was the oldest computer Luke had ever seen, with a screen that couldn't be more than twenty-four inches. Incredible, Luke thought, picturing the wall screen in his clean, comfortable pod room. There was a sagging stained blue sofa, a few big floor cushions and four cheap resin table chairs. Luke wandered over to the window that reached almost from ceiling to floor. From there he could see the credit point across the road.

'You're really high up here.'

'Yeah, twenty fifth floor. Keeps us pretty fit.'

'So you saw me from here?'

'Yeah, I happened to look out and there you were. Then I saw Sheldon and Co. sidling up and thought there'd be trouble and of course, my girl Saskia here tagged along to make sure I was all right.' Zach turned and grinned at the thin girl with the strange long hair and Luke tried to imagine her rescuing anyone from boys like Sheldon.

'You don't talk like them,' Luke said

'Not likely,' Zach laughed, 'It's called Black Country, or some kind of remnants of it. It used to be a real accent, apparently, but now it's like a badge, certain families, certain groups.'

Luke nodded, 'A bit like Beauts and Messers.'

'Ha! Never heard of Messers.'

'That's what I am, into messing with things, technology and science and stuff.'

'Ha! I like that. Guess I'm a Messer too, then. That's how I keep body and soul together, fixing stuff, computers, gadgets, whatever people want.'

Luke nodded. He wanted to ask how old Zach was, living here in his own flat with his girlfriend, but he didn't want to appear rude.

'You hungry?' Zach asked.

Luke thought about the chicken sandwich he'd bought in the mall. It seemed like a hundred years ago now and the thought made him feel light headed. He might never see his friends or family again. He could no longer call anyone or access the net. He felt too disoriented to be hungry. He sank onto the sofa and stared blankly up at Zach. Saskia hovered behind him looking more nervous, 'Are you all right, Luke?'

Luke shook himself, 'Sorry, I was just thinking…'

'Too late for that, mate,' Zach said jauntily. 'Have you eaten at all today?'

'A sandwich,' Luke said rallying himself. He'd made his decision and now he'd have to see it through. 'Perhaps food would be a good idea.'

'Great. You like curry?'

'Fine.'

Zach moved to the kitchen end of the room and began taking pre-packed food packages out of an old-fashioned fridge and loading them into an even older looking microwave oven.

'Coke or water?' Saskia asked.

Luke wondered what coke would taste like, a drink that wasn't allowed in his exclusive pod or school, but decided to stick with water. Saskia arranged plates of micro-waved curry on the table and pulled heavy brown curtains across the long window before she invited Luke to sit down. Luke tried not to look shocked by the food, an orange-brown mess of vaguely curry scented gravy with lumps in it. He closed his eyes and forked up the food, so unlike the freshly prepared meals he had eaten all his life.

'Good curry?' Zach asked, washing his food down with a long draft of coke.

Luke nodded, 'Very good, thanks,' he lied graciously.

When they'd eaten Saskia took the plastic dishes to a sink and started to wash them by hand. Luke shuddered at the thought of all the bacteria. Zach moved to the computer and flipped on the monitor, 'Thought we should check out whether there's any news on you, mate.'

Luke sat up straight as though electrocuted. 'Me?'

'Yeah, mate, what did you think? That they're just going to let you run off and not mention it, son of the biggest artist in the city, probably in the country?'

Luke put his head into his hands. 'If I'm on the news what about people who saw me? People in the station and the café and that kid Sheldon and his gang?'

'The most likely thing is that none of those people will download news. Most people round here aren't exactly clued in. If someone does recognise you, they'd still have to contact the Regs. Even if there's a reward on finding you, most people would think twice before inviting the Regs into the area, Luke. They don't exactly tread lightly round here.'

In the kitchen, Saskia paused with a half washed plate in her hands and shot Zach a look, 'We'll be fine, babe,' Zach smiled broadly in Saskia's direction and she went back to the dishes. 'Anyway,' Zach said in Luke's direction, 'You won't catch Sheldon watching news and his lot are the only ones who saw you near me and Saskia.'

'And they don't know you came back with us,' Saskia put in from the kitchen.

Despite Zach's reassurances, the thought of the news made Luke's stomach churn and he thought Saskia's face was taking on a sickly green tinge as they watched. He felt his panic rising again; the way it had on the train and in the street when he realised exactly what he'd done. He wished he could go inside his own head and check the news in private, but he needed Zach's old-fashioned, cheap monitor to link to the world now. Luke stared at the screen where a smiling virtual presenter talked the audience through Luke's last traced movements. 'Malik's personalised tracker implant was later recovered from a monorail line in the Wednesbury area.'

Luke sighed with relief. At least they didn't know where he'd got off.

'A monorail guard later identified the absconded teenager as a young man seen in Telford station at around 1 p.m.'

'Shit!' Luke began to pace the small room.

'Malik's pod Guardian, Claudia Mason, has appealed to the teenager to return...'

Claudia's face, looking so pinched and ill that she was almost unrecognisable flashed on the screen. Behind her Kyle sat on a sofa looking dazed and pale.

'Shit!'

Luke only just made it to the toilet before he vomited out the glutinous microwave curry. His throat was raw with acid from the regurgitated food, but his stomach lurched again, adding bile to the foul smelling mess in the toilet bowl.

From behind him Saskia's hand reached for the flush mechanism. 'Here, drink this,' she offered, handing Luke a glass of cold water.

Back in the living room Zach had switched off the monitor. Luke slumped into the sagged blue sofa and rubbed his forehead with both hands. 'Do you want a pain-killer?' Saskia asked gently.

Luke shook his head. 'Thanks, I'll be fine.'

Saskia shot Zach a look, but they stayed quiet, hovering close to Luke.

'Do you think I should go back?' Luke asked almost inaudibly.

'No!' Zach and Saskia spoke together.

Saskia sat down next to Luke and Zach pulled up a resin chair. 'You said you had to get out. You had to save yourself. What good would it do going back?' Zach asked quietly.

'But all the trouble I've caused... My friends, my dad, even Claudia. They're all going to be questioned and…' Luke trailed away. He pressed balled up fists into his eye sockets to keep the tears back and took a deep breath.

'Look, mate, they were already going to be questioned. Think about it. If they had you down for all that labelling and medicating malarkey, they'd be looking to blame anyone and everyone you knew. You don't need me to tell you how they operate.'

Luke looked up and nodded.

'Your dad's a big-shot artist. He can look after himself. And your friends aren't daft. They know what to say to distance themselves. What you've got to do is make the best of it. If they find you it was all for nothing, right?'

Luke nodded. 'Yeah, you're right.'

Saskia scooped her long frayed ropes of hair back from her face, 'You'll need clothes,' she said, 'and a less noticeable hair style. How do they do that?'

'There's a tiny implant that creates directional static. It…'

'Okay, that's technical enough,' Saskia grinned, 'so we have to stop the static.' She looked towards Zach, eyebrows arched in question.

Zach puckered his face, considering for a moment, 'Get me a metal comb, babe.' Saskia left to rummage in another room and Zach stood up and stretched.

'There you go,' Saskia handed the comb to Zach. She really admires him, Luke thought.

Saskia watched intently as Zach attached wire to the comb and tied it to a metal plumbing pipe that ran

132

along a wall, 'Thank goodness for shoddy old buildings with exposed pipe work, eh?' Zach grinned, 'Okay, Luke, we just need your head now. Squat down here and run the comb through your hair a few times. Well, maybe quite a few times.'

Luke shot Zach a questioning glance, but walked towards the tied up comb and squatted down.

'It'll be earthed see?' Zach said.

Luke grinned, 'Yeah, you're right.' He ran the comb through the halo of black hair repeatedly until his arm began to ache, but the hair finally settled back into its old shape. Saskia held a small, scratched mirror up for him. He still looked too well groomed for the Subs, but at least he wasn't such a screaming advert.

'It's brilliant, Zach,' Saskia enthused. 'I'll get you some different clothes tomorrow, first thing,' she said, turning back to Luke.

'Good,' Zach agreed. 'Saskia works in a second-hand shop. She can easily put some stuff by. Can you bring it back during your coffee break? He needs to get gone as soon as possible. He can have my old rucksack.' Zach turned towards Luke, who let the comb drop. He shook his arm free of the stiffness that had set in from combing for so long and stretched out of the squat position.

'Your trainers are way too fancy really, but anything we get for you won't be a proper fit and you might need to be able to move fast at some point. We'll try for baggy trousers and hope no-one notices,' Zach concluded.

Luke walked over to the window and pulled back the curtain. Outside it was dark, the streets and houses lit up by lights, people going about their lives. Luke wondered where he would be this time tomorrow and shivered. He let the cheap brown curtain fall back and walked over to the sofa to slump next to Zach. Saskia curled on a floor cushion nearby.

'Do you know where you'll go, Luke?' she asked gently.

'The Standing Ground,' Luke said before he'd thought about what he should say.

Saskia and Zach exchanged a quick glance.

'The what?' Zach asked, incredulous.

'The Standing Ground. It's this place in North Wales where…'

'We know what it is,' Zach said, dropping his voice as though they were being listened to, 'but is it even a real place?'

'What do you mean? Of course it's real. I met a girl from there. Online I mean.'

'Yeah, but was she real?'

'Yeah, she said so and she had these weird clothes…' Luke trailed away. Surely Alys was real?

'Well there's rumours, of course,' Zach said tentatively, 'sites that come and go with stories about life before E-Gov and old legends, something about someone called King Arthur…'

'But they could be fake, Luke,' Saskia put in. She wound her fingers around one of the ropes of dark hair and bit her lip, 'It could all be a way of drawing out

134

opposition to E-Gov. Some of the sites are really weird. They make you feel as though you're really there, not just hi-tech virtual stuff, more than that. Some people think only E-Gov could set up sites that powerful.'

'Some people think that's what's really out there in North Wales is camps. Prison camps like that island they were going to send you to, or worse,' Zach finished.

'But Alys,' Luke scrunched down into the lumpy sofa with his head in his hands. For a moment, he felt like he might be sick again, but pulled himself upright, 'It exists,' he said as definitely as he could muster, 'Alys is out there in The Standing Ground and I'm going to find her. Anyway, what else am I going to do?'

Zach shrugged and Saskia looked tearful, but she leant towards Luke and forced a smile, 'Just be careful, Luke, and if you find your Alys, let us know.'

Zach nodded, 'Yeah, mate. If that place is really out there you have to find a way to get in touch. This is big, mate, really big.'

When Saskia and Zach left him alone to go to bed, Luke tried to settle into the blue sofa to sleep. It was lumpy and the spare blanket that Zach had brought him had a damp, musty smell. He wondered what it was like in Zach and Saskia's room. How old were they? Perhaps only two or three years older than him, but here they were with jobs and a home, taking care of themselves. Luke drifted to sleep, wondering what Alys was doing at this moment, miles away in The Standing Ground.

In his dream he was in a forest. Snow was falling and the trees were bent under the weight of it. A shiver ran down his spine as someone's hand touched his. He couldn't see anyone near him, but he thought he caught the glint of a small red stone, like a single red eye in the shadows.

'Stand still. The trees listen to me. They will hide you. Just stand still.'

It was Alys's voice. Luke turned, but there was no one there. Then he heard her voice again, far off, but speaking in a language he couldn't understand. Welsh, it must be Welsh, he told himself, turning again to try to see her.

He woke suddenly. The room was dark and he was alone, but Luke couldn't shake the feeling that someone had been standing over him. Luke shuffled over to the screen and flicked it on, turning the sound down so that he could just make out the words of the newscast.

'Several reports suggest that the absconded teenager, Luke Malik, has headed north after last being seen in Telford. Mr. Danver Horace, Chief Regulator of Birmingham, who is leading the high profile enquiry, believes that the teenager, who is thought not to be in his right mind, may be heading for the border in the hope of crossing into Scotland. There have been a number of sightings of Malik north of Salford. The authorities warn the public not to approach Malik.'

'Salford?' Luke said out loud. He shrugged and flipped off the screen. Well something was going in his favour. He should try to get more sleep.

Luned

In my dream I move silently through a strange building. I move along a corridor and into a room where Luke is asleep, hunched on a sofa, tossing and restless. I rest a hand on his forehead and speak a blessing.

In another room the shadows are illuminated by an alarm clock. I can make out the shape of two people sleeping. The boy's arm is flung over the girl's bare shoulder and the girl's long ropes of hair are splayed out around her. I kneel by the bed and reach for something. My hands find a cheaply made back-sack and open a small pocket in its lining, gliding the zip noiselessly. I take the band from my finger, the ring I have worn for as long as I can remember, in this life and in lives long gone. The plaited twists of red Welsh gold and the small red stone catch the glow from the alarm clock.

'Go safely,' I whisper and drop the ring into the pocket of the back-sack.

I am Luned, mistress of the moon, who serves Vivian, the lady of the lake. I am Creirwy, daughter of Ceridwen of the White Song, who dwells under Lake Bala. I am the shape shifter who will guide the boy through Annwn. The moon is growing full, the Solstice is approaching and soon I will know my full power.

15

Luke gagged on the first spoonful of microwave porridge from the bowl that Saskia set in front of him. He closed his eyes and breathed deeply. You have to eat, idiot, he cajoled himself. He concentrated on thinking about Alys and took another spoonful, trying not to notice the glutinous lumps that caught in his throat. Saskia was grinning at him when he opened his eyes.

'Sorry about the food, Luke, I don't suppose it's what you're used to.'

Luke shrugged and grinned back. 'It's fine, really, it's just…' he struggled for something polite or at least half true to say.

'Crap,' Zach offered good-naturedly.

Luke grinned again, 'I don't think this is the time to be choosy, though.'

'You're right there,' Zach agreed, 'I've got to get to work. Got a washing machine to mend this morning down at the launderette. Saskia will be back around ten with the clothes.' Zach paused and coloured, 'So I suppose this is good-bye and good luck, mate…' he muttered.

Luke stood up and offered Zach his hand, 'Thanks for everything, Zach. You probably saved my life.'

Zach shook his head and coloured more, but he took Luke's hand and shook it, then suddenly pulled Luke to him and clapped him hard on the back, 'You look after yourself, Luke Malik, and when you find that Standing Ground, we want to know about it.'

Zach let go of Luke and fumbled in the pocket of his baggy beige trousers. He handed Luke a card that read, 'Zach Hindmarsh, Household Maintenance and Plumbing' with an email address and mobile phone number written underneath. Luke nodded, 'Absolutely. You'll be the first to know.'

Zach and Saskia left together. Luke waited for the click of the door then sat on the sofa, closed his eyes, and tried to steady his mind. He was still disoriented by how much he had lost: his familiar site that he could no longer mentally walk through to connect to the web was only a memory; the mind calls to his friends already seemed dream-like. He felt shaky thinking about it, but it was done. He shook himself and opened his eyes. He had to learn to live on the wits left to him now that he had none of the benefits of mind enhancement.

A noise at the end of the corridor roused Luke. He glanced at the wall clock, ten past nine; surely it couldn't be Saskia back yet. He crossed the small living room and peered down the corridor. Outside the heavy front door with its two large bolt handles that enabled Saskia and Zach to triple lock their door from inside as well as outside there was a banging noise, the thud of something heavy against the metal cage. Luke tensed.

'If yow're in there, 'Indmarsh, yow'll get a bloody good hiding when this door gives way! Yow see if yow don't.'

The thudding stopped and Luke breathed heavily into the silence, which changed again to a mechanical whir. 'Yow in there, 'Indmarsh? I've got a bleeding chain saw yow know, so yow may as well open the bleedin' door.'

Luke felt the ground spin under him. For an insane moment he thought about climbing out onto the balcony, but he knew that he would have no chance of escaping that way. He crept along the corridor and veered off into Saskia and Zach's bedroom. He felt uneasy entering their private space. It smelled of old fashioned incense and was strewn with cushions and throws in saturated colours, Saskia's work no doubt. Luke glanced round the room trying to combat the urge to regurgitate the awful porridge he'd made himself eat for breakfast. The bed was a divan with no space underneath. There was a wardrobe in one corner, but it looked old and wobbly and wasn't large enough to crawl into. Should he try to hide or let the aggressive visitor in and at least save Saskia and Zach from having their door torn down? Think, moron, Luke told himself.

'I can bloody hear yow in there, 'Indmarsh! Open the bleedin' door. Yow give me the rent now or yow're for it!'

Shit, Luke moaned to himself, think of something. He edged towards the front door.

'Saskia and Zach are out at work,' he called, trying to sound unperturbed.

'And who the hell am yow, then? Those scum-bags sub-letting?'

'No. No. I'm just a friend. I'm not staying. I'll tell them you called.'

The voice outside didn't reply immediately and Luke held his breath, hoping the man had gone away. Something slammed against the cage door outside and Luke heard a wail of pain, then a sob, 'Well, well it's 'Indmarsh's girly. Yow better 'ave some money for me, girly, or I might 'ave to take payment in kind if yow know what I mean.'

Luke shouted before he had time to think, 'Leave her alone!'

'Yow gonna make me, scum bag?' The man laughed and Luke heard Saskia struggle against the door and mutter something inaudible. Then, 'Shit! Shit, girly, that hurt, that did! Yow bite me again and yow'll get the hidin' of yowr life. Yow mark me.' The door rattled again and Saskia whimpered, 'Right girly, yow open this door and we'll just sort out my rent one way or another.' There was a pause. Luke froze, waiting. 'Yow deaf, girly, or just daft? Open the bleedin' door now!'

Luke heard fumbling, the jangle of keys, then the graunch of metal as the cage door and bolts juddered open. The front door swung inwards, and the man pushed Saskia ahead of him so that she stumbled into Luke, who was still motionless in the dim corridor.

The man was short and stocky, square-faced and in his forties. He had unkempt grey hair and a paunch tightly wrapped in a grey nylon t-shirt under a cheap suit jacket that was shiny with age. Grey Paunch sneered at Luke and let out a long, slow whistle. 'Well, well. Look at what we've got. Just visiting, eh? Yow're that kid off the news, amn't yow? Yow've done sommat to that fancy hair, but yow're him all right. Now isn't this interesting? And them Regs seem to think yowr in bleedin' Salford.'

Luke froze.

'Yow're looking a bit green around the gills for a Beaut,' Grey Paunch sneered, 'Now let's all sit down nice-like and work out what to do next, shall us?'

He pushed Saskia roughly down the corridor ahead of him so that she toppled into Luke. Luke steadied her and she whispered, 'Sorry, Luke.'

Luke shrugged and managed a weak smile. In the living room Saskia and Luke huddled onto the two ends of the sagging sofa, looking anxious and defeated. Luke thought of offering Saskia's landlord his money, but there was nothing to stop Grey Paunch from taking the money and still handing him in. There would be a reward, after all.

Grey Paunch grinned and swung the hammer he'd been using against the door from his thumb and fat first finger, letting it rock like a pendulum. 'So tell me, what's a Beaut like yow doing with scum-bags like 'Indmarsh and his girly?'

Luke bit back the urge to object to being called a Beaut. 'Nothing. I mean, I never met them before. I met them in the street. Zach helped me out of a bit of bother and I persuaded him to let me stay the night and get me some clothes. They needed the money, that's all. They don't know anything about me.'

Grey Paunch caught the swinging hammer in his palm and aped banging the hammer against his own hand: once, twice, a third time. He paused and looked at Luke again with the same sneering grin. 'They know yow're not from round here, Beaut. What's yow're name? No, don't tell me…' he let the hammer fall into his palm again and again, 'I remember… Luke, in' it? Luke Malik? Yowr Dad's some big-shot artist in' he?'

Luke nodded glumly.

'Got rid of yowr PTI they said on the news. That right?'

Luke nodded again.

'So yow got a plan?'

Luke hesitated.

'Yow may as well tell me. Yowr not gowing anywhere without my say so, anyway. And yow wouldn' want me getting narked and takin' it out on the girly here, would yow? Yow know what I mean?'

Luke let out a long breath. He could feel Saskia hunching further down into the sofa. 'I'm making for Wales. I heard there's people there. People who don't…'

'The Standing Ground?' The sneer in Grey Paunch's voice rose to pure derision, 'Bloody fairy story for kids

143

or silly sods who's daft in the head. Nothing up there but wasteland after the battles with E-gov, if yow ask me.'

'I'm willing to find out, either way,' Luke said, working to keep his voice even.

'Yow got money?'

Luke nodded.

Grey Paunch nodded too. 'Well, I'll tell yow what, Beaut. Yow pay me an' I'll take yow as far as Llangollen. I've got rents to collect over there, see, so I can get through the Regulation Points no problem and if yow're under the seat no one'll be the wiser without the PTI going off.'

Luke gazed back, uncertain, looking for the catch.

'We got a deal, Beaut?'

Luke glanced at Saskia. She looked pale and close to tears. 'You'll leave them alone? Saskia and Zach, I mean?'

Grey Paunch leered at Saskia, 'Give yow my word, Beaut.'

Luke could feel his stomach tense, but he was helpless.

'You go, Luke.' Saskia said, almost inaudibly. She turned towards Grey Paunch defiantly, 'Don't you hand him in, Karl, or Zach'll have you!'

Grey Paunch grinned, 'Well, Beaut, looks like it's all settled. We'd best be off then. My car's right out back.'

In the corridor Saskia picked up a limp black plastic bag, 'You should take the clothes, Luke, you'll need a

144

change for after Llangollen. I've got the back sack in the bedroom.'

Karl pulled the carrier bag from Saskia before Luke could take it, rooted in it and handed it back to Luke, 'Get the back sack then, girly. Us 'aven't got all day yow know.'

The journey, crammed under the seat of Karl's car with the back pack under his head, was the most uncomfortable Luke had been in his life. The movement of the car made his head spin with pain and he felt dehydrated and dizzy. Every jolt translated itself into a pain somewhere along his spine and the shoulder he was lying on became first numb and then jerky with shooting pains. Luke closed his eyes and wished he could call Kyle, but the thought of his friend only made him feel more alone and miserable.

When the car engine ceased, Luke tensed. He heard a door open and listened to Karl's loud, nasal voice, full of confident patter, then another quieter voice, a Regulator, Luke guessed. A tensed muscle in Luke's neck shot into spasm suddenly and he curled up, wrenching his foot against the shell of the car. He held his breath.

The quieter voice was louder now and closer. 'Are you carrying something in the back, Sir?'

'Nothing in there, officer.'

Another spasm pulsed down Luke's spine and his leg jerked again.

'I think you'd better let me take a look in there, Sir.'

Luke heard the back door of the car being pulled open and Karl's voice rising to a rapid whine, 'Yow don't need to look in there, officer. Yow can see for yowrself there's only me in the car.'

Luke's leg went into full spasm.

'Could you lift the back seat for me, Sir?'

'I don't think it lifts, officer. Been jammed as long I've 'ad this car.'

'Sir, if you could just…'

Luke heard a dull thud and the beginning of a scream that was strangled by a thick gasp almost as soon as it began. The seat above Luke sagged towards him in the dim half light.

'Shit!' Karl's voice.

Luke tensed. He could taste his own fear. He heard the squeak of something heavy being dragged across the shiny plastic surface of the seat above him, then a dull thud, another thud and the sound of Karl, breathless and further away, intoning curses.

Luke waited for what seemed like a long time, listening for new noises. He thought he might have heard a faint splash, then another, louder. The seat was dragged back above him and Karl loomed over Luke, while he blinked, disoriented and weak with cramp and fear.

'Bloody stupid Beaut! Yow couldn' even 'old still for a couple of bloody minutes! Now look what yow've made me do!' Karl reached in and grabbed Luke, pulled him out of the awkward hole beneath the seat and dragged him out of the car. Luke caught the tang of something metallic in the air. Karl slapped Luke upright against the body of the car, let go and wiped an arm across his sweat covered face.

'Yow just bloody look what yow've made me do!' Karl jabbed at the air in the direction of the verge, towards a steep bank and ditch. Luke peered. He couldn't make out anything in the ditch, but he could see the smeared trail of blood between the car and the grass verge. He glanced back into the car. The wrenched out seat was smeared in something sticky and dark. Luke looked down at himself. The blood was smeared thickly down his trousers and clung in globs to his trainers where Karl had pulled him through the trail. Luke heaved and a thin smear of bile dribbled from his mouth. He wiped his sleeve across his face and tried to steady himself. He glanced up at Karl, whose grey nylon t-shirt was spattered in aerosol dots of blood, almost invisible. Blood was already drying in brown stains on Karl's hands.

Karl spat towards the ditch, pushed past Luke and threw the back pack into his arms. 'Yow better run, Beaut. Yow'r wanted for murder now and they'll 'ave tracked this pig's death already. They read the bloody scum-bag's vitals while he works!'

Luke felt the ground rock beneath his feet. Karl was still talking, ranting, but Luke couldn't make out the words. He saw Karl reach for the hammer under the car and felt a cold, sick certainty that he was about to die. Karl shot him the sneering grin and swung the hammer. Luke flinched and closed his eyes, paralysed except for a trace of pee that escaped involuntarily. He heard Karl groan and fall and opened his eyes. Karl was on the floor, writhing and groaning, drool coming from one side of his mouth and his left arm twisted at an odd angle. Luke tried to make sense of what he was seeing. Why had Karl swung the hammer into his own arm?

Karl spoke breathily, 'Now look what yow've bloody done, Beaut,' he rasped, 'Broke my arm when I tried to stop yow killing that bleedin' Reg.'

Luke took off like a bullet. He only looked round once. Karl had dragged himself into the car and was making a call on his mobile, calling in the terrible thing that had happened, no doubt; but he wouldn't be telling it like Luke remembered it. Of course the Regulator's station would already know that their officer was down, but they wouldn't suspect this. They would be puzzling over how someone whose vital signs were constantly monitored and whose health was kept in peak condition could possibly go down without warning. Luke couldn't ever remember hearing about a Regulator being killed on duty; it would be a national incident.

Luke could feel the cold air burning in his lungs. His legs felt less steady with every thud of his expensive, blood stained trainers against the frost bitten ground. He ran over an open field that was spattered with frozen remnants of muddy snow. From there he turned into a wood, grateful for the cover, but crashing and stumbling through a narrow trail where his feet sank in mud and grey snow-thaw and leafless tendrils of bramble clawed at his skin and clothes. He emerged on the edge of a housing complex. Neat rows of narrow houses; a district of service sector workers, Luke guessed, not people like Saskia and Zach, people with implants, but lower grades than the one he'd had himself until yesterday.

It was almost dark. At least night came early in December. Luke turned away from the houses and followed the sound of a stream. He splashed water onto his face, cupped more in his hands and gulped it down. It was so cold it almost burned in his throat, but he hadn't drunk since breakfast time. He poured more water into his mouth and gulped hard at the sharp stab of iciness. When he could drink no more, Luke began pulling off his soiled clothes. He shivered in the cold, unused to being exposed without thermal fabrics to insulate him. He dipped his t-shirt in the stream and used it to wipe at his trainers. When he'd erased the blood he began burying the soiled clothes under a nearby boulder. His teeth were chattering by the time he pulled on the clothes from the back sack, but he felt energised by the water and the burst of purposeful activity.

Luke stood still, trying to imagine what to do next. He had a sudden image of Karl, cooking up his story for the Regulators, his nasal voice speeding up as he invented lie after lie.

'Yow won't believe how relieved I was when that young Regulator pulled us over. He'd been sat behind me for miles with that hammer at my head, forcing me to take him to Bala. Had some mad story about some renegades up in the hills past there. Ranting he was, officer, crazy. Course the Regulator identified him at once. "Step out of the car, Mr, Malik, please," he says. And the kid got out, but he had the hammer behind his back and I suddenly realised just 'ow mad he was. I dashed out quick as I could, like, but I was on the wrong side of the car, yow see. By the time I got there, Malik had done it. One blow at the back of his skull, straight through it went. He had to pull to get the hammer out again and that's when I lunged for him, but he was young and fit. He rounded on me and I felt this blow across my arm and passed out with it. When I came to, he'd got the body and the officer's bike down in the ditch and he was nowhere to be seen. They never said on the news how dangerous he was. Never seen anyone that vicious in all my years and I've seen some things, officer, some things as could make yow'r hair curl. But him…'

Luke shook himself. There was nothing he could do about Karl and his lies. He had to keep going, he had to get to the Standing Ground, but he didn't even know where he was or what direction to head in. He stood still. The sun had set now, ahead of him, so that had to be west, the direction he needed. It was a start, but at night, what would be his chances of keeping on course, especially in woodland? Luke hunched down onto a boulder and buried his head in his hands. The clothes Saskia had brought him provided no heat despite feeling bulky and awkward. He shivered and unzipped the rucksack, but he knew already that he was wearing everything Saskia had given him. A pocket in the inside lining caught Luke's eye and he pulled it open, wondering why he was bothering. There was something there. Luke dipped in a hand and pulled out a ring that seemed familiar. Where had he seen it? Luke closed his eyes and reeled from the loss of memory and net access, but forced himself to concentrate. It was the ring on one of the fountain statue projections in Nazir's garden. It was the same ring that Alys had worn on the website.

What was going on? Was the whole thing a trick after all? Was Nazir further into E-Gov than Luke suspected, after all? It would explain the access his father had. Perhaps Alys wasn't real. How could a girl in a primitive renegade society build a website where he could smell blood or be scorched by a dragon's breath. If Alys was a creation, then she was Nazir's creation and it would explain the statue of her projected in the fountain. What was the point of going on?

Luke cradled the ring in his hand and clutched it tight. He curled up small on the hard ground and began to sob.

Myrddin Emrys

I have been in despair and known what it is like to wander, lost, imagining the worst. Artur has also known despair. When he was tricked by Margawse and realised that he had slept with his own sister; when his baby daughter died and he had no time grieve and knew that Gwenhwyfar would never forgive him; when he discovered Gwenhwyfar in the arms of his son, Medraut; when he faced Medraut in his last battle at Camlan. Despair makes us think everything is at an end, but it is not. Even after death there can be hope.

He has the ring, though he does not know its power. Now his guide will go to him.

16

Alys woke feeling anxious. It was only 5.a.m according to her bedside clock, but she knew she wouldn't go back to sleep. She shuffled across her room, tensing against the cold, and wedged herself into the low, narrow window seat overlooking the garden and stream. It was snowing again, thick swirls of milky crusts, heavier this time, Alys noted. Something niggled at the back of her mind, but she couldn't capture the thought. She pulled on her warmest trousers, the thick fleece lining soft against her shivering skin, and layers of tops underneath her heaviest sweater. She flicked on her computer and pulled her chair in close. What was it that was waking her earlier every morning and then eluding her memory?

Alys stared at her latest workings on the encryption for a long time before giving up in frustration, 'Stupid!' she said out loud She paced her room and came back to sit in front of the screen. She stabbed at the keys to close the encryption file and then connected to the web, unsure of what she was looking for. Without thinking she typed 'Luke Malik' into a search engine and a list of sites appeared, not encrypted government files, but news stories. Alys followed the first link.

A picture of Luke flashed onto Alys's screen, his black hair fanning out in a lop-sided halo around his smooth, oval face.

'Tuesday 19th December 2075: Teenager Luke Malik today absconded from the prestigious Bullring School in central Birmingham, later removing his PTI in an attempt to evade being returned to his pod and school. Malik was experiencing behavioural problems related to a suspected severe medical condition, which was in the process of being diagnosed. His Connexions Counsellor, Natalie Thorpe, confirms that staff and pupils at the Bullring School were becoming increasingly concerned about the teenager, who was beginning to show signs of Questioning Authority Disorder and Inappropriate Behaviour Syndrome. Malik had been in conflict with tutors and had even shown physical aggression.

Tutor Dominic Simons, spokesman for the school, said, "We first became concerned for Luke's well-being when he began to question the curriculum and his lack of access to detrimental and damaging information. Clearly, no right thinking person would want to access harmful knowledge, and we acted promptly to get Luke the help and support he needed. I can only imagine that he must have been much sicker than we realised and that he must have been hiding his symptoms for some time. Our only concern is to find Luke so that he can receive the treatment he needs to live in his own and everyone's best interests. Luke is a very confused and unwell young man and we urge anyone who sees him to contact their nearest Regulation Point immediately."

Malik is the son of the late writer, Vivian Raven, and prominent installation artist, Nazir Malik. Concerns have been raised about the possibly inappropriate relationship between the influential and sometimes controversial artist and his teenage son, but Mr. Malik was not available for comment. Claudia Mason, Luke Malik's pod-Guardian at the expensive Bullring pod-1 expressed shock at the teenager's disappearance, describing Malik as "an intelligent and sociable young person who has never previously given any cause for concern".

Others, however, are not so surprised. Bradley Hunter, son of the banking tycoon, Harrison Hunter, was recently the target of an unprovoked assault from Malik and said that Malik's peers were united in feeling that it was only a matter of time before Malik would be involved in some major incident unless he got immediate treatment.

Plans are in place to treat Malik at the top E-Gov treatment centre for de-formed teens: Serenity Island. Staff at the centre assure us that they deal with difficult cases on a daily basis and are proud of their record of a 100% re-form rate. "We provide the kind of loving discipline that lost and ill teenagers like Malik are crying out for," said a spokesperson for the Island centre, "Children come here with the most entrenched and life-debilitating disorders, but our mixture of cutting-edge medical intervention and safe structures enables every one of them to get back on track. We never give up on anyone no matter how long it takes. There is no child who cannot be re-formed at Serenity Island."'

Alys followed more links. There had been a sighting of Luke in an unconnected suburb of Birmingham, and then the trail had been picked up going north, though precise location was hampered by the lack of the PTI to track Luke down. Alys clicked on the next link. A picture of an overweight man with a sweaty face and a broken arm set in a resin bandage half filled the screen.

'Karl Everett is the last person to have seen the absconded teenager, Luke Malik. Mr. Everett, a landlord from Telford, was surprised by the runaway when he attempted to collect rent from one of his buildings. Malik, who Regulators now warn is extremely dangerous, hijacked Mr. Everett as he was about to enter the building. Mr. Everett was threatened with a hammer and forced to drive Malik to Wales. The incident ended in tragedy when a Regulator recognised Malik and stopped the car. Malik brutally attacked the officer and Mr. Everett, leaving the Regulator dead and Mr. Everett bleeding and wounded.'

'No!' Alys said loudly to no-one. She shivered and closed down the web page. Outside the snow was deepening rapidly and she felt exhausted. She lay down on her bed fully dressed, pulled the top quilt over her and fell asleep wondering where Luke was now.

In her dream she was with Luke in a barn on the edge of a wood. She uncurled his fingers, took the ring from the palm of his hand and worked it onto his little finger.

'Wear this, Luke, and they can't see you. You'll be safe now, but I won't leave you alone...'

'Alys. Alys, cariad.'

Alys woke to her mother's voice. She rubbed sleep from her eyes and sat up.

'I came in earlier, cariad, but you looked so asleep. You're still dressed. Are you all right, Alys?'

'Mam! Mam, I've got it!'

'Alys?'

Alys raced to her computer and began typing numbers, her fingers stumbling over the keys in their haste. Gwen came up behind her and watched the screen. After a few minutes she laid a hand on Alys's head and brushed it lightly down to Alys's shoulders, 'I'll send Owain up with some breakfast, cariad.' Gwen tip-toed out of the room and shut the door carefully.

Owain arrived ten minutes later with a tray. He put it down on the deep slate of the window recess and sidled up behind Alys.

'Have you really got it, Alys?' Owain's voice was a taut whisper. He peered at the formulae and shook his head, 'Is it going to work?'

Alys bent over the keyboard and typed harder, sighed deeply, and spun round to face Owain. She grinned at him, stood up and threw her arms around him in answer. 'Has Mam left, Owain? I need a lift to Emrys's.'

'What about breakfast, Alys? And what about the snow? It's going to get deep today. I don't think even Mam is planning on going any further than Blaenau today.'

'I have to see Emrys, Owain. This is it. It's really it, and Luke's in trouble. We've got so much work to do…'

'Luke?'

Alys flushed, 'He's this boy I met.' Alys flushed deeper as Owain raised an eyebrow. 'Stop it, you oaf! He's living under E-Gov. He found one my sites when I was squatting. He's run away and they say he's killed a Regulator, but he can't have. He needs help and…'

Owain held up his hand. 'Slow down girl. Look, print that stuff out and email Emrys. Then eat something or at least have a hot drink. I'll take you to Emrys's, but we'd better pack something. We might be gone a while.'

Alys flung her arms round her brother for a second time, and then began following his instructions. Owain left to pack a back sack for himself and returned a few minutes later looking anxious and red-eyed.

'Are you okay Owain?' Alys looked up from stuffing warm clothing into an overnight bag and paused with a fleece half folded.

'It's Taid, Alys, he's… he's…'

Alys nodded, 'I know,' she said quietly, 'I guessed a few days ago. Is he worse?'

Owain nodded.

'Does Dad know?'

Owain nodded again, 'Dad's in the kitchen. He's... he's crying, Alys. Dad is...'

Alys dropped the fleece and put her arms round Owain. She heard him choke back the tears and gripped him more tightly. Owain breathed deeply and stepped back. 'Have you said anything to him? To Taid I mean.'

Alys shrugged. 'He doesn't want to talk, Owain. He says it's his time. Mam says he won't have chemo.'

Owain nodded. 'Do you still want to go over to Emrys's?'

A small noise at Alys's door made them turn. 'Of course she wants to go to Emrys Hughes,' Tomas said. He leant against the door frame. He looked visibly frailer today and his skin had a distinct yellow tinge now. 'You look sharp now, go and finish this maths with Emrys and give me some time with your Dad.' Owain opened his mouth to object, but Tomas held up a frail hand, 'I'll still be here when you get back, boy.'

Owain glanced at Alys and she nodded. 'I really think I've got it, Taid,' Alys said trying to sound normal and cheerful.

Tomas smiled, 'There now, Owain, how's this for a day to remember? Dewi Jenkins away plying his arguments in Brussels to get us a country while Alys and Emrys crack the codes. Synchronicity is the word, I think.'

Owain grinned, 'It is Taid.'

Tomas turned and began to shuffle back to his own room, already becoming unsteady with the pain. Owain sprang after him, only to be waved aside, 'I'm not dead yet, look,' Tomas forced himself to smile, 'I'll do for myself while I still can, Owain.'

Owain bit his lip and nodded. He came back into Alys's bedroom and slumped on the bed. 'This is quite a day, then?'

Alys sat down next to him, 'Yes,' she said quietly.

'Okay then,' Owain roused himself and smiled broadly, 'Let's do this. Let's make some history of our own while Dewi is doing his thing in Brussels.'

Alys smiled gratefully and pushed the green fleece into her bag, 'I'm ready.'

Owain drove cautiously out of the village and onto the New Road that had been new now for the last seventy five years. The wide sweep of the descending hill was already covered in snow, but the New Road was broad and well maintained and there wouldn't be any problems getting as far as the turning for Maentwrog. At the turning Owain gripped the wheel hard and listened for the sound of the snow chains on the narrow road up past Tan-y-bwlch. The snow was thickening, but the vehicle was in good shape, maintained by Cen ap Rhys, whose family had run the local garage since before Tomas was born. They finally pulled round the last corner into Rhyd and Owain gingerly inched the car into a lay-by a few yards from the terrace of cottages where Emrys lived.

'Thanks, Owain.'

Owain nodded, 'No problem. You go and knock. I'll get our bags.'

Emrys opened the door before Alys could knock and ushered her in. She stamped off the snow before pulling off wellingtons and Owain did the same behind her while Emrys took their bags.

'I think you're right, Alys. I've got the computer doing some crunching now, but I think you're right. Genius. Bloody genius you are, girl!'

Alys made a mock bow and sat down on the plump red sofa that was pulled close to the wood burning stove. Owain perched on the arm of the sofa.

'I'll put the kettle on while the computer's chugging away. I emailed Gethin Parry and he's going to run a secondary check for us. He'd come down if he could, but I think Nain Parry might go today. He can't leave her now.'

'Mam said it wouldn't be much longer when she saw her on Monday,' Owain agreed.

'So it's all happening today.' Emrys said in Owain's direction, 'Nain Parry's the end of an era, and maybe today's the beginning of the end for E-Gov into the bargain, not to mention whatever Dewi Jenkins is up to at the minute.'

'So we better get that code cracked and bring the government down while we're still part of their country,' Owain grinned, 'Clock's ticking, Emrys.'

Emrys shot Owain a returning grin and went to fill a kettle. Alys sighed with relief at the peace between Emrys and her brother and leant towards the stove to soak in its warmth. She hoped the truce would last. While they drank tea Alys told Emrys and Owain about the newscast on Luke.

Emrys leant on his arm and rubbed his chin, 'Sounds like he's in a tight spot Alys, but something tells me he didn't kill that Regulator.'

Alys shook her head emphatically, 'I don't believe it either. How could one boy overpower a Regulator and a grown man? There's something shifty about that man, I know there is. And all that stuff from his school, that's all because he refused to toe the line, Emrys. They make these syndromes up. They make it seem like it's an illness to disagree with E-Gov.'

'I agree with you, girl, but he's out of there now and on his way here. I have a feeling he'll have the help he needs, Alys, we just have to trust him and play our part.'

'He's right, Alys,' Owain put in. 'Luke's fighting E-Gov just like we are. The least we can do is make it worth his while and get this code cracked.'

'Exactly,' Emrys agreed.

'The computer should have finished crunching,' Emrys said when they'd finished drinking steaming mugs of tea, 'Let's go and see what we've got. If we're right and it cracks the encryption we can use your friend Luke as our test. See if we can erase some files and make him a bit more invisible than he already is.' Emrys winked at Alys and she had a sudden image of the dream she'd had early this morning. She looked down at her hand and realised that her ring was gone, the ring that she never took off. Alys nodded and smiled back. Of course Luke would be invisible to E-Gov.

'If that works then the next stage is to launch our virus.'

'Virus?' Owain asked.

'We've been developing it ready for this day,' Alys explained breathlessly, 'Once we can get into E-Gov data files we can infect all their communication channels: E-Gov news, E-Gov information services, E-Gov instructions to citizens. We can throw them into chaos.'

'Brilliant!' Owain laughed, 'This I want to see.'

Upstairs Emrys's spare room was crammed with technology. Owain whistled admiringly as he stepped in. 'Pretty serious kit in here, isn't it?'

'Every magic-making thing I can get my hands on,' Emrys confirmed 'That lot there runs Y Tir's economy.' Emrys motioned towards a wall of computers and black boxes winking with red and green lights, 'All our trade: computer software deals, every item that comes in or goes out on the ships at Caergybi.'

Owain nodded, 'And this lot?'

'That's strictly number crunching. In the old days, before they could chemically link single walled nanotubes this much computing power could fill a whole building,' Emrys said proudly, 'and there's a lot more technology out there Owain that we haven't even got our hands on yet. We need more technology for The

Ground, and if I have my way, today is the day we start to acquire it.'

Owain nodded again, 'Yeah, the medical stuff,' he said quietly, 'but it'll be too late for Taid.'

'Tomas? Tomas is ill?'

'Liver cancer,' Alys's voice came out as a hoarse whisper.

'Bloody hell! Well, no time to lose then. At least Tomas Selwyn should get to see what it's like to live in freedom again.'

'What can I do?' Owain asked.

Two hours later Alys and Emrys sat back, tearful and exhilarated, 'Bloody genius!' Emrys repeated his mantra of the day.

Owain came into the room, 'Dinner in five minutes. I hope it's all right mind.'

Alys smiled broadly at her brother, who wasn't someone who normally involved himself with how food got onto the table. 'I'm sure it will be wonderful,' she reassured him.

'You've done it then?' Owain checked.

'Too right we've done it. Before we eat I want to get into our friend Luke's E-Gov file. Ready?' Owain and Alys huddled further towards the screen almost holding their breath as Emrys launched the first sabotage assault, 'And go! I'm in! Bloody brilliant! Now then, let's see – everything must go, I think.' Emrys began cheerfully deleting a set of files, including the latest sanctioned news transmission files:

164

'Regulation Officers are today continuing their search for the run away teenager, Luke Malik. Authorities have warned that Malik is extremely dangerous and should not be approached. Any sighting should be reported immediately. Any information leading to Malik being safely returned to re-formation facilities for his own welfare will be generously rewarded. Malik was last seen on the perimeter of Llangollen's Deacon District and is believed to be heading west.'

'Is that what he looks like?' Owain smirked at Alys and winked at Emrys, 'Bit pretty isn't he?'

'Shut your mouth,' Alys quipped, 'And don't you say anything, either,' she warned Emrys, her colour rising.

'Moi?' Emrys feigned innocence. 'Well, take a last look, Alys. Until you see him in the flesh of course.' Emrys pressed the last delete option on the menu, 'Luke Malik is no more. At least as an E-Gov file. Didn't I tell you I had my own invisibility spell, girl?'

'So what next?' Owain asked, hopping from foot to foot like a child before a party.

'Well, we can't erase every file by hand like that, we'd be here forever and they'd shut us down before we could get much further. So now we launch Excalibur.'

'Excalibur?'

'Alys's name for our cunning virus. It was the name of King Artur's sword.'

'Nice. So it'll wipe all the files at once?'

'I'm going to do a global call for the encryption code then a global open command with Alys's lovely new magical algorithm and simply direct the virus to everything that's found. It's speed that matters, which is where my powerful baby comes in. Let me show you.'

Emrys began punching in instructions and within seconds lists of files scrolled onto the screen, Emrys skimmed the titles as the list grew, page after page.

Emrys nodded, 'There we go: eighty million citizen files, all the news outlets, curriculum control...' he trailed away, scanning the last screen to appear, 'Hmm... Ah...'

Alys leaned in further, 'Bastards!'

'Alys!' Owain objected, then changed track, 'What is it, Alys?'

'They've got a deeper level of encryption, the sly so and sos.'

'So we can't...?'

'We can still do plenty,' Emrys re-assured. He hit a key hard, 'And we will. There he goes: Excalibur is live and free.' Emrys turned towards Owain, 'What it means is that we can't do the whole thing. We can shut down a whole swathe of their data bases: personal files, work records, school records and programmes, Connexions, news control, Internet monitoring, even the PTI control software. We can cripple them, but they've kept a bit in reserve: inter-E-Gov communications, policy decisions, international and defence files and, sadly, the Regulation Authority database, which means of course our man Luke is not quite out of the woods yet.'

'Can you crack the second code, Alys?' Owain asked.

Alys groaned, 'Depends on the nature of the beast. If it's a five-twelve-bit encryption it could take us years again.'

'Food!' Emrys commanded. 'Come on, Alys. Owain has cooked and we are going to eat. Excalibur will have cut their outer defences to shreds by the time we've had lunch and we need to stretch and think.'

'I wonder how Dewi is getting on?' Owain ventured over lunch.

Emrys swallowed a mouthful of potato, 'Well, if anyone can sell our case it's Dewi Jenkins and everyone thinks our chances are the best they've ever been.'

'Will you still break the second encryption? I mean if we're independent?'

'Independence won't happen overnight. As long as we get the encryption broken before official independence it's sabotage, not war,' Emrys said reflectively.

'And we will break it.' Alys said with quiet determination.

'So what will you call the next virus?' Owain asked, breaking the tension that surfaced whenever Dewi Jenkins or Brussels was mentioned.

'Artur,' Alys answered instinctively, 'Taid is going to live to see Artur return. He told me that whenever

167

we stand up to evil that's when Artur returns. That's what we're doing. Holding back the darkness.'

Emrys and Owain nodded in unison.

'Brilliant food, Owain.' Alys said warmly.

Emrys was right. By the time they had eaten and returned to the computers Excalibur had done its work. Alys trawled through news sites: they were all down or carrying single pages with bland messages that said there was nothing to worry about, normal service would resume soon.

'In their dreams,' Emrys crowed. 'Now for our next trick.'

'What's that then?' Owain asked, exited again.

'A little back up virus that Alys has aptly named Glyndŵr after your very own namesake. This one will do some major squatting for us. We've got web pages ready to go: history, critiques of E-Gov, arguments against the General Will, exposés of E-Gov abuse. We've got about a dozen different sites and Glyndŵr will randomly generate copies of one or other of them freely throughout any site that we've emptied of content: all the E-Gov citizen information sites and news sites, for instance.'

'I could get into this computer stuff,' Owain said admiringly.

Emrys smiled, 'They'll lock us out eventually, but they've got bigger problems with all their databases down. This will keep them fighting on too many fronts. Anyway, this is the bit where people have to do something for themselves. They get the information and have to decide what to do with it.'

'Yes,' Owain agreed, 'And now we wouldn't be deserting them if we broke away and got independence, would it?'

Alys smiled.

'I suppose you've got a point,' Emrys said. 'Just let me get Glyndŵr launched and I'll check my emails, see if there's any news from Dewi. I need to email Gethin anyway, let him know how we're doing and find out how Nain Parry is.'

Emrys typed rapidly again, 'Done.' He opened his email programme and clicked on a mail that was flagged with an exclamation, 'From the Council no less.'

'Yes!' Owain leapt into the air. 'Yes! Yes! Yes!'

The three of them danced in a circle, laughing until Alys sat down suddenly and burst into tears.

'Alys! Alys are you all right?' Owain was at her side.

Emrys squatted down in front of her and wiped a hand gently across her face, 'Quite a day eh, cariad?'

Alys nodded and sniffed, 'Yes.'

'Are you upset about the independence?' Owain asked anxiously.

Emrys and Alys shook their heads simultaneously, 'No. No, I'm really happy. It's just all so much. Breaking the encryption and Taid and Luke and Nain Parry and independence on top of all the rest. I think I'm going to burst with it all.' Alys smiled and sniffed again, 'I'm fine really.'

Luned

When I woke this morning it was like surfacing from a deep lake into the sudden realisation of myself. Luke has the ring and with it I can lead him safely through Annwn, as I've always led the lost. I will be there with him as he crosses the wasteland. And I will be here too – working the magic that Myrddin Emrys and I have laboured over for years.

The moon will be full tonight. The eve of the Solstice and my power will wax with it.

17

'Are you all right?'

Luke looked up. The girl who had spoken was about his age, dressed in jeans and a plain, dark sweat-shirt; not the most expensive clothes, but memory fabrics none the less.

'You don't look very well,' the girl prompted.

Luke rubbed his head. He ached everywhere. His body felt so stiff he wondered if he could still move and it took a few moments for him to remember where he was before the events of the previous day flooded back with sickening clarity. He stood up cautiously, wincing with pain in every muscle and the girl flinched back, 'You're that boy...'

Luke expected her to turn and run, but she stood still, holding his gaze. Something about her eyes reminded Luke of someone he knew.

'Luke Malik,' Luke said grimly, 'And I'm not a murderer.' He watched the girl watching him. If she was afraid she was hiding it well. 'You don't need to worry,' Luke added for good measure.

The girl shook herself almost imperceptibly. 'I'm not worried. So what happened?'

Luke groaned, 'Long story, very long story.'

'I'm not in any hurry,' the girl said.

Luke groaned again, 'Listen, I need to move on. I...'

'Are you hungry?'

'Ravenous,' Luke said, realising what the pain in his ribs was.

'My pod's nearby. Don't look like that. It's Winterval Eve. The Guardians have taken everyone out on some theatre trip. I told them I had stomach ache. There's no one else there.

'But the security will pick me up.'

'Thought you'd got rid of your PTI?'

Luke grinned, 'Yes. I haven't got used to the new me yet, though.'

'Come on then. You're in more danger out here than in my pod. I'm Elin by the way. Elin Williams.'

'Pleased to meet you Elin Williams,' Luke returned, hoping he would be still be pleased to have met the girl in an hour's time. They left the almost derelict barn where Luke had spent the night and walked down a track towards a small town. 'Where am I exactly?'

'Corwen,' Elin told him, 'the last outpost of civilisation.'

'Seriously?'

Elin nodded. 'The road hasn't been maintained past here for over forty years and no one is supposed to walk further than Druid a few miles on from here. The old road splits there, but it's just a pot-holed track in both directions.'

'And beyond that?'

'Old places where no one lives like Bala and a few deserted villages. Then it's the mountains and no one knows what's beyond those.'

'And no-one tries to find out?'

'We're told that there are E-Gov security stations and labs over there with restricted access. Highly restricted. Some people think that's a story and it's really prison camps and don't want to risk poking their noses into E-Gov business. Others think that it's a land of myth and magic, but either way no one goes there.'

'Point taken,' Luke agreed, 'But aren't there other stories?'

'The Standing Ground?' Elin asked. Luke nodded and Elin let out a snort of laughter, 'They tell us it's all fairy stories. The free Welsh up in the mountains speaking a language that's been around for two thousand years. They say it's nothing more than stories for silly kids.'

'That's what I intend to find out.'

Elin stopped walking and gazed at Luke. 'You might not be a killer, but you are tough.'

Luke grinned, 'We'll see.'

Elin led Luke through a gap in a hedge and into a pod compound. At the door a mechanical voice greeted Elin, but seemed unaware of Luke's presence. He could hardly believe it was possible. Being inside a pod, especially one decorated for Winterval, reminded Luke of his family and friends. He felt dismal and alone, despite Elin's cheerful chatter as she filched food from the kitchen. In Elin's podroom she sat quietly while he ate hungrily.

'Okay, tell me everything,' she said as soon as Luke finished the last mouthful.

'What do you already know?' Luke asked warily.

173

Elin gave him a potted version of his so called illness and murdering tendencies, and Luke corrected her as she went along, carefully skirting over any mention of how Saskia and Zach had helped him.

'I'll show you the news sites if you like,' Elin offered when Luke had finished telling his edited story.

'Thanks.'

Elin ran a hand over her wall screen and touched the menu pad that appeared. A news screen scrolled into view, the pale green and familiar logo of the Regulation News Service.

'Weird,' Elin commented.

"Regulation News Service regrets that a freak weather condition has caused problems with transmission. This will be corrected shortly and normal news transmissions will soon resume. There is no cause for concern."

'Never seen anything like that before,' Elin added, but Luke couldn't help noticing her broad grin.

'Me neither. Try another one.'

'All down. Weirder and weirder. There's been a bit of snow, but mostly slush, so where's this so called freak weather?'

'Got me there. Anyway, at least they can't spread any more malicious lies about me for now. Perhaps it's a good time for me to get on my way.' Luke stood up.

'While it's light?' Elin queried. 'Loads of people know what you look like and there's a reward out for you.'

Luke sat down again. 'When is your pod getting back?'

'They're going for a meal after the theatre. They won't be back till after dark, around six o'clock. It's dark by 4.30 so we can be long gone.'

'We?' Luke stood up again.

'What, you think you're the only one who ever thought life's crap under E-Gov?'

'No. No, of course not, but you said yourself we don't even know if The Standing Ground is out there. I could be walking into E-Gov's hands and even if I'm not I might get lost on top of the mountains and wander about till I starve to death.' Luke remembered the despair he'd felt last night before he found the barn, but he didn't believe any longer that Nazir was betraying him, that it had all been a trap. He felt a calm certainty that he would find Alys, as though he'd been reassured by dreams.

'We'd better take some food then,' Elin said with determination, 'And I'll see if there are any clothes to fit you in the laundry. Those things you're wearing are really odd and …'

'And what?'

'They kind of smell.'

Luke laughed, 'Yeah, I know. They don't have memory.'

'Where did you get them?'

Luke bit his lip, considering. 'A couple helped me in Telford.'

Elin nodded, 'The Subs.'

Elin left Luke alone while she investigated the laundry. She returned with two full sets of clothes, the kind of clothes poorer kids wear, standard memory fabric, up-to-date, but not expensive or too fashionable. Luke changed in Elin's washroom while Elin packed a spare set of clothes and some of her own things into Luke's back pack.

'I'll go and see what food I can find now,' she said when Luke emerged from the washroom. Now that he was clean, he felt more in control again, despite the dull ache that still throbbed through his muscles and the headache that lurked just beneath his eyes.

Elin returned with a second back pack filled with food and drink, heavier than the first. Luke glanced at the time display beside Elin's bed. 'One o'clock,' he said out loud, 'Three and a half hours till we can leave.'

'It's dusk at four. If we go back the way we came, we can get out onto a track behind that barn you slept in. There are a couple of derelict villages down that way, Cydwyd and Llandrillo. I'll leave a note to say I'm feeling a bit better and have gone for a walk, so they won't start looking till curfew.'

'Great,' Luke said, 'but you really don't have to come with me. I mean you should think about...'

'I have,' Elin said flatly.

'Why?'

'Why did you leave?' Elin's voice was angry now.

'I told you why. I had to do something, They were going to ship me off to Serenity Island to be medicated and re-formed.'

'Well maybe I have to do something too.'

'What, you're in trouble?'

'I didn't say that.' Elin sat down on her bed. She took a deep breath and faced him defiantly, 'I don't really belong here. I can't tell you more than that, but it's the truth. I won't slow you down. I can be your guide.'

Luke sensed that it would do no good to argue. 'All right.'

Elin relaxed. 'Let's have another look at the news. See if they're back online.'

'Weirder and weirder,' Elin said when they tried to log on to the first news service.

'Elin look!' The screen shimmered into a new page, a yellow gold page with a red dragon rampant across the top.

Welcome to Y Tir – you have arrived at a history page sponsored by the Glyndŵr Resistance of The Standing Ground. Enjoy this page and please visit us again soon.

'Bloody hell! They've broken E-Gov's encryption codes, Elin.'

'Yes,' Elin said.

'She's really out there,' Luke went on, awed.

'She?'

'Alys. I met her online. She said she was from The Standing Ground. I'd never heard of it before, but now I'm sure she's real.'

Elin smiled at him and Luke felt again the sense that he'd met her somewhere before.

As they left the pod it occurred to Luke suddenly that Elin's PTI would put them in danger. Ahead of him Elin walked through the door and stopped dead.

'My PTI.'

'I was just thinking that. We should take it out, I'm afraid.'

'No, that's not what I mean. Watch.'

Elin walked back through the door into the pod and back out again.

'It's not working!' Luke almost shouted.

'Your friends with the encryption cracker are doing a thorough job.'

'We should test it on something else,' Luke cautioned. 'Can you access your own site?'

Elin closed here eyes, 'Yes.'

Luke grimaced, 'Depends what they've done. The virus might have been targeted to destroy E-Gov control signals and systems, in which case your enhancement features could still be in tact. We need something that tests more specifically.'

'We could just take it out,' Elin offered.

'I haven't got plasters and it hurts like hell.'

'Still...'

'Think, Malik!' Luke said to himself.

'There's a shop down the road,' Elin volunteered, 'I'm not missing yet. I could go and buy a magazine. That way I can see if my PTI triggers their door.'

'Sounds good. I'll meet you through the gap in the hedge.'

Elin was back in ten minutes. 'Everyone's PTIs are down and the man in the shop said there's a lot more going on than that. You were right. The rumour is that a virus has broken through E-Gov encryption and is wiping out all kinds of files. I don't think they can track me.'

'But your mind enhancement still works?' Luke asked, incredulous.

'Yes.'

'What about email monitoring?'

'It's done through my PTI…'

'But not in the Subs,' Luke interrupted, 'How do they monitor email in the Subs? They intercept it at the hubs, don't they? They use key words to trigger monitoring. If the systems that control PTIs are down then what's the chances of the monitoring systems being taken out as well?'

'Pretty high I should think.'

'That's what I thought. I need to send an email. Can you do it for me?'

Elin nodded, 'Let's get to the barn first. I don't want to be out in the open so close to home.'

Inside the derelict barn where Luke had spent the previous night Luke pulled a crumpled card from his pocket. He noticed the brown stain on it that must be blood from the Regulator, but if Elin saw it she didn't ask any questions.

'Okay, send it to Zach Hindmarsh at this address,' Luke handed Elin the card, 'Tell him Luke's on his way to The Standing Ground and that he and Saskia should set off while there's chaos.'

The track out of Corwen had once been a minor road. They passed a rusted sign with a faint outline of numbers barely visible, 'B4401,' Luke read, shining the torch that Elin had given him onto the mangled sign.

They passed the second deserted village about eight kilometres down the track and stopped to drink. The road veered right towards hills in the distance. They walked at a steady pace, hardly speaking, concentrating on avoiding pot-holes in the cracked and ruined road beneath their feet. After another five miles the incline increased and they slowed their pace further. 'We're not going very fast are we?' Elin asked.

'Hard to say, but we're moving in the right direction,' Luke said. His spirits had risen since finding The Standing Ground's web page squatting over an E-Gov news service site.

'Look,' Elin pointed along the road. Even in the darkness the long lick of a lake was clearly visible shimmering in the early moonlight. They reached the lake and stood for a while watching the dark water.

'I think we should turn right here,' Elin said confidently, 'Both roads go West, but only the one to the right goes North.'

Luke nodded, 'I think that must be right,' he agreed. 'Are you all right to go on?'

Elin punched Luke good naturedly. 'Is that sexism, Luke Malik?'

'No, of course not, I just…'

'I'm perfectly all right. Do you want more water?'

'Thanks. What time is it?'

'Nearly eight o'clock.'

'What time's your curfew?'

'Eight in winter unless I have a pass, which I don't of course, so that means they'll start looking for me, but I don't think we need to worry. There's so much chaos back there.'

'Yes, but we should keep going.'

As the road climbed the tattered patches of snow merged together and gave way to more heavily sprinkled hillsides. The road steepened sharply as they walked and fresh snow began to fall. They walked on doggedly, heads bent against the driving blizzard, silently following the torch beam along the rutted road. Luke was grateful for the smart fabric of the stolen trousers, without it he'd be soaked and frozen to the bone, he thought.

It was two hours before they reached a second lake, a straggle of derelict farmhouses along its length and the snow deepening by the minute. Luke shivered despite the smart fabric. He didn't want to admit that he was exhausted, but he could feel his legs stiffening with every step.

'Do you think we should take a break?'

'If you need to,' Luke replied, hoping that Elin would say that she needed to stop.

'Or if you need to,' Elin teased. 'You're allowed to get tired you know. You've been on the run for three full days and you've been through a lot.'

'Maybe I could do with a breather,' Luke agreed. 'We could see if there's any shelter in that house we just passed.'

They retraced their last steps and pushed their way through a rotted door that had once been painted green. Inside the smell of damp and mould hit them, but the oak floorboards seemed solid. Upstairs snow melt dripped through the ceiling in patches, but the slate ground floor seemed unperturbed by the years of neglect. Kitchen cupboards hung limply from the downstairs walls and wind howled down the long cold chimney.

Luke jammed the outer door as closed as possible and pulled the inner porch door tightly shut. In the corner of the kitchen was a hay bale. Elin pulled it in front of the cold fire and began pulling it apart. 'Find some wood, Luke,' she commanded.

Luke scanned the room and headed for the kitchen cupboards. 'I'm not sure how dry it is,' he said, pulling a door from its hinges, 'How are we going to light the fire?'

Elin grinned, 'I'm sure I'll have something in the back sack.'

Luke looked at Elin admiringly. She looked tired and her mousy hair was damp and clinging to her round face, but she kept going. Luke began cracking the wooden door against an old kitchen surface while

182

Elin spread a thin thermal picnic blanket over the straw.

'More good thinking,' Luke said, grinning, 'You're pretty organised, aren't you?'

'You don't know the half, Luke Malik.' When Elin laughed Luke realised who she reminded him of. He shook himself. Get a grip, Malik, the whole world reminds you of Alys at the moment, he told himself.

They sat on the blanket, insulated against the chill of the slate floor and ate the food that Elin had packed nearly seven hours before. 'So, do we go on or stay out of the cold for the night?' Elin broke the silence, 'No-one knows I'm with you, so I can't see why they'd come in this direction.'

Luke nodded, 'From the look of those E-Gov websites, they've got more problems than a couple of run away teenagers to keep them occupied.'

'They certainly have and I'm not sure I fancy our chances in the wind and snow out there all night, thermal clothing or not.'

'I know. To be honest, I can feel my muscles seizing up. I'm not sure I could keep going even if I tried.'

The fire had gone out when they woke next morning and they rose stiff and unrefreshed. Outside the snow had deepened and the wide road was only barely distinguishable from the surrounding slopes. They followed the curve of the lake, heading west. They made slow progress, forcing their tired, cold muscles along the badly decayed, snow covered road. Luke was

183

glad of Elin's quiet company. If he was alone he thought he might sit down in the snow and let himself give up, but with Elin he would keep going until they found shelter. They walked without speaking, stopping occasionally to pant out streams of moist breath into the biting wind or to sip at water that burnt their throats with cold. Luke kept himself going by thinking of Alys ahead of him across the hills. They ploughed on for three hours more before they rounded a steep bend. Across a bridge they saw a sign post ahead of them, 'Croeso – Trawsfynydd.'

'Welcome to Trawsfynydd,' Luke said jubilantly, catching his ribs as he panted in the icy air.

'How do you know that?'

'It's Welsh. It's your ancient language, Elin. Alys said that to me when I met her online. Croeso, I mean.'

'So we're here?'

'We're here!' Luke grinned.

Myrddin Emrys and Nazir

The two iridescent cauldron discs are almost three metres across, held ten metres apart by tubular pillars which wind around one another in a helix pattern like the spiral of human DNA. When I flick the remote the tubes fill with coloured light, red and blue. There is an intake of breath from the crowd in Victoria Square. After today's chaos it is more important than ever that the festival opens without a hitch. The faces of petty E-Gov officials look pinched and anxious.

Slowly, the colour inside the tubes coalesces into globes of light, becoming paler, and soon the spheres are transparent, like bubbles at a children's party. The crowd make out images at the centre of each orb and I can feel them holding their breath and craning forward for a better view.

It takes a long time for the applause to die down, but eventually Denver Horace manages to call order and make way for the mayor to introduce me. I know I won't get much of my speech out before the Regulators make a dive for me to drag me off the stage and take me into custody. But there will be nothing there for them to arrest. The illusion will vanish. Nazir Malik and Emrys Hughes will be one and the same person, as I was before I met Vivian. I will be at home in Rhyd with Alys, who, like me, has sent out an illusion to guide Luke to us.

18

They left Emrys's computer sending out the Artur virus the next morning. The last part of the puzzle came to Alys as she slept. Emrys soon crunched the new numbers for her with his prized computer that filled a whole wall of his spare room. It was done. E-Gov would never recover from the second assault, not in any form that could control every citizen. With the work finished Alys was itching to get home to her family for Solstice Day and even keener to be there to meet Luke.

'You launched your installation?' Alys asked Emrys while Owain was upstairs in the bathroom?

'I did indeed. It's only a shame that my illusory self wasn't there to see the looks on their faces when I vanished before their eyes.' Emrys put the palms of his hands together and pushed away so that the tips of his fingers remained touching, a characteristic gesture of Nazir.

'It will be a lot for him to take in, Emrys.'

'It will, but at least it will explain all the coincidences he's been noticing. Now, we should get you home and see how things are going there.'

Alys jumped out of the car almost before Owain had switched off the engine, 'Steady on, girl!' Owain called, but he was grinning. Emrys opened the passenger side door and the two of them followed Alys up the path to Tŷ Meirion. Inside, the kitchen seemed to be bursting with the smells of Gwen's cooking.

'Happy Solstice!' Geraint greeted them. He held a glass of something golden, toasted Owain and Emrys and took a deep draught. 'Come in Emrys. Let me get you a glass of whisky. Dad's been saving it since he was born apparently. The only whisky made in Wales.'

Emrys edged further into the warm kitchen and smiled at Tomas Selwyn who was ensconced in a chair by the wood-burner, 'Don't mind if I do, Geraint. Nice colour on it, Tomas.'

'Pour him a tidy drop now, Geraint,' Tomas said smiling though his pain. Alys took the glass from Geraint and handed it to Emrys, sniffing it as she did, 'Bit strong, Taid!' she laughed, 'Is it really as old as you?'

'Older. My parents bought a case the year the distillery opened and kept a bottle by for each of us as we were born. Finally seems like the day to open it, what with cracking the code and getting the green light on independence all in one Solstice.'

Taid looked exhausted from so many words and Alys thought he looked as pale and yellow as the whisky, but she smiled warmly. 'Emrys hasn't only been busy cracking codes,' Alys launched in. 'Apparently when he was away in E-Gov he had a whole other life – as someone called Nazir Malik. It was his father's name. He has a son who is on the run from E-Gov and we're expecting him today.'

Alys stood back while her family began to fire questions all at once in Emrys's direction. She could see now that Nazir looked exactly like Luke, perhaps a little darker. She couldn't imagine how she had ever missed the clues, but that was the power of illusion; the art of misdirection, she smiled to herself, conjuring up an image of Luke on the last leg of his journey.

Across the kitchen Gwen was bustling with roasting trays filled with chicken, duck and vegetables and Alys watched Emrys sidle up to his old friend to help her load the trays into the oven.

'You heard Nain Parry passed on this morning, Emrys?' Gwen asked.

'Yes, I had an email from Gethin before we left home. He said she was very peaceful at the end, thanks to you.'

'No more than she deserved, Emrys. I'm just glad she went before the cancer got to her brain. It's terrible when they change and don't know you at the end.'

Emrys glanced over at Tomas anxiously.

'Tomas'll be fine,' Gwen said, 'He's not having chemo so it'll take him before it can spread that far. It's one blessing at least. The world really is changing.'

'At least he's lived to see it change and toast it with his whisky.'

Gwen smiled ruefully. 'At least,' she agreed.

'Want a hand, Mam?' Alys asked at Gwen's side.

'You can get some cutlery out, cariad, and warm a stack of plates. He sounds like a resourceful young man, Alys, this son of Emrys's.'

'He is Mam,' Alys agreed

Alys almost dropped the plates onto the table at the sound of a knock at the door. She darted across the room and flung open the door. Luke was there, being guided to the door by Eleri Jenkins with a motherly arm on his shoulder.

'Ah, Alys, cariad, I've found your guest, look. Came in on the Trawsfynydd road about eleven this morning he did. I gave him a quick bite and a hot drink and got him straight over to you,' Eleri said, smiling warmly, 'but he's very worried about his companion. Seems she went missing just as they got to Trawsfynydd. I sent Jac and the boys out to take a look, but nothing so far, I'm afraid. I can't think...'

Alys smiled. 'It's fine Mrs. Jenkins. Let Mr. Jenkins know she's okay. I had an email from Elin. She had somewhere else she had to be.'

Eleri Jenkins looked puzzled, but nodded, 'If you're sure, Alys.' She shepherded Luke into the kitchen. He hung back feeling oddly shy until he noticed Nazir.

'Dad! How... I mean ...'

Emrys put his palms together and bowed, smiling, 'A long story, Luke, a very long story, but it will unfold soon enough. For now let me just say that I've had a double life for some time. Here I am Emrys Hughes and I'd like to introduce you to my closest friends and our compatriots in the struggle.'

Emrys began making introductions. Luke wanted to ask about Elin, but when he glanced at Alys he knew the answer. It was Alys who had been his guide for the

189

journey, even though he couldn't fathom how she had done it. Alys caught his eye and Luke flushed and ducked his head.

Emrys stood behind him and put his hands on Luke's shoulder 'And this, of course, is Alys. Alys Eluned Selwyn.'

Luke took Alys's outstretched hand nervously and then, on impulse, dropped it and threw his arms around her. He stood back. 'Pleased to meet you at last Alys Eluned Selwyn and Happy Solstice!'

Jan Fortune-Wood is an educationalist, poet, novelist and editor. Her previous novels for adults are *A Good Life* (Bluechrome Publishing, 2005) and *Dear Ceridwen* (Cinnamon Press, 2007). She is also the author of several books on education and parenting, the most recent being *Winning Parent, Winning Child* (Cinnamon, 2005) and a collection of poetry, *Particles of Life* (Bluechrome Publishing, 2005). She is currently working on a second poetry collection, *Knot-work*, and completing a novel written as a sequence of prose poetry microfictions, *Stale Bread and Miracles*, to be published in 2008. She lives in North Wales with her husband and four children and is currently learning Welsh.

Author's Note: Whilst the characters and events of this novel are completely fictional the ideas for the brutal setting of Serenity Island are based on research about a real place sparked by Decca Aitkenhead's article, 'Tranquility Bay', Sunday June 29, 2003, *The Observer*. Similarly ideas about future government directions are in part inspired by real moves towards increasing surveillance and intrusive databases of civilians.